OLD HAUNTS

Eastwind Witches 11

NOVA NELSON

FFS Media

Publisher's Note: This is a work of fiction. Names, characters, places, and incidents are a product of the author's imagination. Locales and public names are sometimes used for atmospheric purposes. Any resemblance to actual people, living or dead, or to businesses, companies, events, institutions, or locales is completely coincidental.

ISBN: 978-1-7330264-7-5 (FFS Media)

Cover Design © FFS Media LLC

Cover design by Molly Burton at cozycoverdesigns.com

Old Haunts, Eastwind Witches #11 / Nova Nelson -- 1st ed.

www.novanelson.com

Contents

Chapter 1   1
Chapter 2   8
Chapter 3   14
Chapter 4   26
Chapter 5   31
Chapter 6   40
Chapter 7   44
Chapter 8   52
Chapter 9   62
Chapter 10   72
Chapter 11   79
Chapter 12   85
Chapter 13   91
Chapter 14   102
Chapter 15   109
Chapter 16   117
Chapter 17   126
Chapter 18   131
Chapter 19   136
Chapter 20   143
Chapter 21   151
Chapter 22   161
Epilogue   172

First-Realm Problems   175
You're Invited...   177
About the Author   179

OLD HAUNTS

Eastwind Witches 11

NOVA NELSON

Chapter One

With those first hot and sticky days of early May rolling through Eastwind, witches, weres, fauns, leprechauns and the like were making every excuse to remain indoors. And what better way to beat the heat than with a refreshing drink at the pub?

Some people liked to have a solid excuse for whiling away the hours in Sheehan's Pub, but I never felt the need. I worked hard and when the day was up, so long as there wasn't any pressing ghostly business to attend to, I got to spend my days however I wanted. That was the rule, as far as I was concerned.

And if that free time included Donovan Stringfellow and a cold pint, even better.

It was Saturday night, and the stars had aligned (I'd nudged some of them into place, if we're being honest) just such that I had free time, a sweating pint of Sheehan's finest ale in my hand, and my heart-stoppingly hot East Wind witch boyfriend by my side.

The pub was packed for the annual scufflepuck

tournament. Fiona Sheehan and Kelley Sullivan, both of whom were managing to keep up with drink orders by the skin of their teeth, had cleared out all the tables and chairs in the main area, scooted the existing scufflepuck table into the middle of things, and added one more for good measure. If you didn't get a seat on one of the stools at the bar, it was standing room only.

Donovan and I didn't get seats at the bar. But that was okay because it gave us an excuse to stand shoulder to shoulder, his arm wrapped around me as we enjoyed cold drinks and observed some of the first-round play, waiting for our turn to compete.

I'd missed the tournament last year, too busy juggling my time between waiting tables at Medium Rare, ogling my hot boss, and, oh yeah, adjusting to the new reality of being a witch who could see ghosts. That was a shame, though, because from what I'd heard, Tanner was quite a lot of fun to be around during the event.

And yes, now I've mentioned Tanner. I probably should have held off on that to convince you of just how well I was moving on.

Seriously! I was!

It'd been just about six months since he'd disappeared, and, okay, fine, I still thought about him sometimes. What was he doing? Was he okay? Had he started a new life already? Did he think about *me* much?

The pain of losing him was still there, but not being one to do things only halfway, I'd been working hard on the grieving process to speed things along. The sooner I moved on and accepted that my days no longer included him, the better my life would be. If that wasn't incentive, I don't know what would be.

Yes, I approach emotions with logic. And it mostly works.

But I knew that while I might stop feeling a dull ache in my chest when he came to mind, I would never forget he existed so long as I visited all the same places around town where we used to go.

Sheehan's was a minefield in that sense. We'd created so many moments together here. This was where he'd saved me from the witch trap set by a doppelgänger, where we'd relaxed together after a shift, where we'd... where we'd... where we'd...

It was also where most of the trouble with Donovan and I had started.

Well, trouble at the time. Now it was more of an origin story for our relationship, which had been going shockingly well the last few months. I say "shockingly" because, well, you know Donovan. And you know me. And you know *us*.

He tightened his hold around my waist and leaned in. "I might need you to do that darkness thing."

I leaned back and looked at him. "What darkness thing?"

"You know, that thing you do where you take away all the light."

"Quenching?" I asked. "You want me to Quench... why?"

He rocked his head side to side as he spoke. "Just, you know, if we're falling behind." When it was clear I wasn't following, he sighed and added, "Whenever the other person is about to make their toss, you Quench the lights and maybe they miss."

I shook my head. "You're unbelievable. That would

3

be using magic, and you know that's not allowed in the tournament."

He rolled his eyes. "Yeah, I *know* that. But who here would even know what was happening? Have you done it in front of anyone?"

"Donovan, I did it *in this very bar*. I'm sure some of the people here tonight were there that time, too."

"You mean with Slash and Seamus and Lucent?" I nodded, but he waved it off with his beer hand, causing a small splash to jump out over the lip of the mug. "Half the people who were there that night have since been arrested, and the other half probably didn't know what hit them."

He had a point, but I had a card yet to play. "Ruby's right over there. She would know what was happening, and if you think she wouldn't report me to Liberty Freeman immediately, you don't know Ruby."

Donovan sighed. "Okay, fine. No Quenching. But maybe you can show it off later, when it's just you and me."

I groaned at his ridiculousness, but allowed him to kiss me. Well, "allowed" sounds like I didn't kiss him right back. I did. And why not? I was already a beer deep, it wasn't exactly a secret that he and I were together, and we were by no means the only couple getting a little handsy in Sheehan's that night. Since it was a Saturday, a lot of the folks there had been drinking since the place opened that morning.

Hey, everyone has to let their hair down sometime, and when you live in such close proximity to beings as deadly as Eastwind held claim to, the need to relax only grew stronger.

Liberty Freeman called our names, and I broke the kiss to realize all eyes were on us. "Oh shoot," I said. "I guess we're up."

Emagine Hopespring, who the town had warmed up to quite well over the past months, would officiate our match as Liberty managed the other table. Both genies were too powerful to participate—pretty much everything they did had a touch of magic mixed in to the point where it was impossible for them to follow the no-magic regulation. So instead, they called the games, and that was probably better anyway—turned out, Liberty's charisma and ability to work a crowd was rivaled only by that of his now fiancée.

Emagine ran through the house rules as a formality as Donovan and I moved to either end of the table. We were up against Landon Hawker and Grace Merryweather, and Donovan had called it an "easy win" for us. I wasn't so certain. Sure, Grace was ready to pop with a baby any minute and cared much more about finishing whatever book she was reading than socializing in Sheehan's, but Landon had been playing this game against the best of the best—Ted and Count Sebastian Malavic—for years. He presented a challenge.

They split up, and Landon came to stand on my side, which meant he and I would be going head-to-head each round, while Donovan and Grace competed for points on their end of the board.

I wasn't terrible at the game. I'd played my fair share of shuffleboard in bars in my earlier years, back before I died and came to Eastwind. And scufflepuck was a lot like that, only with way more minor explosions and slightly different scoring.

Plus, Donovan had conjured up a scufflepuck table in his house the month before and had been training me *well* past the point where it was any fun. Fortunately, I did know one way to bring the practice session to a screeching halt. And I'd used the trick countless times. It involved unbuttoning his shirt, and it worked a little like magic.

But even though Donovan was clearly the more competitive of the two of us, if I was going to play, I was going to play to win.

I nodded at Landon. "It's okay if you're a little rusty."

The North Wind blinked at me. His rosy cheeks were extra flushed from alcohol. "I'm not rusty."

"Sure, sure. It's just that you've been spending a lot of time at home with Grace, and not a lot of time at Sheehan's, getting your tosses in."

He lifted his chin and narrowed his eyes at me. "You're trying to get in my head. I'm not going to let you."

I chuckled. "Fine, fine. I'm just saying, nothing wrong with prioritizing the woman you love and her unborn baby over winning some dumb tournament. So if, say, your tosses all go just a little to the right and into the gutter, I won't judge you for it."

"You've been spending too much time with Donovan," he grumbled, as Emagine handed us the pucks.

Landon shut his eyes, inhaled, seeming to steady himself, and then slid his puck down the table.

For fang's sake. It was a perfect throw.

"All right," I said, "I guess I'm just going to have to win this the good old-fashioned way." I tossed my first puck, and it went too far to the right, into the gutter.

Landon snuck a glance at me, and I said, "Yeah, yeah."

He took his second toss, and though it didn't score as high as the first, it was still solid.

My turn.

But before I went, he said, "Seems like all that concern for me was just you projecting. It's okay, though. I expected you to be rusty. Donovan has always distracted you from more important things."

I paused in my pre-toss routine and straightened. "I don't think I like what you're implying."

He held up his hands defensively. "I'm not implying anything. I think I'm being pretty clear."

Well, look who was suddenly sassy. The meek, nerdy witch who'd been part of my former circle had found a little confidence in the last half a year. Good for him.

I tossed my puck, and it crashed into his low scoring one, causing both to explode and the onlookers to cheer and raise a glass.

"Well done," he said earnestly.

And that's when the match officially started to heat up.

Chapter Two

If the score was any indication, I was only half as good as Landon. Fortunately for my team, Donovan was slightly more than twice as good as Grace and had creamed her every round. But now it was down to the final one.

Donovan's pucks were positioned well across the target, but all Grace had to do to take it into extra rounds was explode a single one of Donovan's four pucks. A smart tap at the right angle would do it.

"You got this," Landon called from our end of the long table. "Just relax."

"So you know," I muttered to him, "telling a woman to relax has never caused a woman to relax."

Grace made her toss, and it looked good, but an unfortunate amount of spin caused the puck to make a slight left, miss Donovan's puck, and fall off the edge of the board into the gutter.

Immediately, I felt bad, that feeling you always get when you beat nice people in a competition. Of course, my delight at making it through the first round in a single-elimination tournament helped carry me through the negative emotion.

Grace, however, didn't seem concerned. And when I turned to look at Landon, I found that he was already hurrying over to her, a big grin on his face. "You did so well," he said, and he took her hand and helped clear a path through the crowd for her.

Donovan appeared beside me. "Nice work, Ashcroft."

He held up a hand and I high fived it.

"Wow, nothing more romantic than being called by my last name."

Donovan shrugged. "There'll be time for romance later. Now's the time for victory."

"We still have ways to go before we're there. How about we just start with a victory drink?"

He pointed at me and nodded his approval. "Good thinking." And then he disappeared through the crowd.

I spotted Landon and made straight for him. The crowd shuffled around as the next teams snaked through to take their place at the tables.

At Liberty's table, Stella and Kayleigh Lytefoot were gearing up for a match against Oliver Bridgewater and Zoe Clementine. And at Emagine's table, Jane Saxon and her sister-in-law Sasha Fontaine were matched up against Stu Manchester and Ezra Ares.

Someone had given Grace a barstool to sit on, and I approached Landon on his other side. "Good game."

He smiled while Grace watched the games with a detached interest and supported her large belly with one hand while holding his with the other.

"You did the right thing," I said, so only he would

9

hear. He looked at me, eyebrows raised with intrigue. I explained. "After you lost, you went straight to her and were supportive."

"Duh," he said. "I love her." He shot her a sideways glance then let go of her hand, promising he'd be back in a second. Then he nodded for me to follow him. Once we had put a few bodies between us and Grace, he grinned like a fool and plucked something out of his pocket. It was a small box, and I guessed what was inside of it before he even opened it and showed me the shiny jewel.

"Siren's song, Landon." I looked up at him. He was still grinning. "When are you gonna do it?"

"Not sure," he said. "Just trying to find the right time."

"Considering she looks ready to pop, you might consider doing it sooner than later."

"I know, I know."

"Let me see that thing again."

He flashed the ring proudly.

"Sheesh. I don't know if I've ever seen a sapphire that big. What do they pay you down in the Catacombs?"

"Enough to keep me working down in the catacombs. And I didn't exactly have anything to spend it on before her, so..."

I nodded. "Makes sense." I slapped him on the back. "I'm happy for you."

His grin faded slightly as he said, "He would have proposed."

"What? Who?"

He leaned closer. "Tanner. He would have... He told me he had a ring picked out."

My mouth fell open. "I... uh... why are you telling me this?"

"Mighty wind, Nora! Because I care about you. And I cared about him. We were in a circle together! I know you both better than most."

"Donovan was also in that circle," I said firmly. "You're forgetting about him."

He set his jaw, a gesture of bravery I wasn't used to seeing on him. "I'm not forgetting about him. And I'm glad you two are happy together, but you know as well as I do that it's not the same. You and Tanner were perfect for each other. You made each other better."

"You don't know what you're talking about," I snapped, feeling bad for it immediately.

"Maybe you're right. So, what, you and Donovan are going to get married?"

"I don't... We're nowhere near that point. But maybe."

"Nora, come on. I'm only telling you this because no one else will. And you were there for me when I thought Grace was..." His voice cracked, then he straightened his posture again and forged ahead. And I, too stunned by his unusual candor, listened. "You'll regret it if you give up on him. When Grace disappeared, and we all thought she was dead... I hate to say it, but I gave up on her for a little bit. And it's the biggest mistake I've ever made. I'm horrified to think that I wouldn't have done everything I could have to find her."

"You thought they'd found her body, though. You thought she was dead. There's no shame in giving up when you think someone's dead."

He glared at me. "You of all people should know that

death doesn't mean much when it comes to separating people. And besides, Tanner isn't dead, is he? Do you really think you can move on with Donovan, build a life with him, grow old together, knowing that you haven't exhausted every option to get Tanner back here?"

"By doing what? Opening another portal and putting the whole town at risk again?"

"Yes!" he exclaimed. "And no one who's been in love would fault you if you did. How can you move on if there's still a chance he could come back to you or you could go find him?"

I was temporarily at a loss for words. But to be clear, it *wasn't* because he'd said anything that had hit an exposed nerve.

Okay, maybe he'd hit a nerve or two. But...

"For fang's sake, Landon! What are you trying to do here? Don't you think it tore me apart when he and Eva left? Don't you think I've dreamed of finding ways to track him down? But it's not realistic!

"We got lucky. That portal that opened in the center of town, those *things* that crawled through it could have killed everyone. The fact that they didn't is, frankly, unfathomable. And you want me to tinker with that magic all over again to find someone who, for all practical purposes, is probably safe and sound in another world? Siren's song! Despite all that, I've finally moved on and am happy again. Why are you trying to ruin that?"

His determination was starting to wither now. "I'm not. I'm just—"

"I know you always liked Tanner more than Donovan. You and everyone else in this dragon blasted town! But what do you expect from me?"

Now he was speechless. He opened his mouth, then quickly shut it again.

"Exactly. You'd better get back to Grace. She'll wonder where you've gone."

He took the not-so-subtle hint and turned on his heel, disappearing through the spectators.

Was this his payback for the trash talking during the match? I couldn't wrap my head around it, and I didn't get a chance to keep trying before someone grabbed my arm out of nowhere, making me jump a foot into the air.

Chapter Three

"Oh, sorry," Bryant Watson said.

I looked down at where his hand was still on my arm, and he quickly let go.

"Have you seen Dmitri?" he asked.

I shook my head. "Who?" I'd worked with Bryant for over a year now at Medium Rare, but I knew very little about him. I wasn't even sure of his age. Werewolves weren't sticklers for birth records other than documenting which pack each was from, so his employment records were no help in estimating his age (I'd checked). Bryant had a youthful face, making him appear around my age or a bit younger, but his full head of gray hair dated him.

"Dmitri Flint."

I shook my head again. "I don't know who that is."

He rolled his eyes. "Right. I forget you never go to Coven events. Dmitri is an East Wind. But more importantly, he was *supposed* to be my teammate for this. We're up next, and I haven't seen him anywhere."

"Sorry," I said. "Maybe you can see if Liberty will push your match back."

He frowned, and a deep crease appearing between his brows.

"Either way," I said. "Have fun. After all, you have the night off." I'd gone ahead and shut down Medium Rare early so everyone could make the tournament. Well, everyone except for the handful of teenagers who waited tables. Greta Fontaine and her gang would have to find other trouble to get up to tonight, since it was adults only in the pub.

Bryant nodded, his concern none the less apparent, and disappeared through the crowd.

Donovan's voice pulled me away from a heated match between the Lytefoots and Jane. "There you are. I thought you might have split to go chase some ghost." He handed me a fresh drink, and I took it gladly. "Nope. Just being social."

"You ready? We're up next."

"Who are we playing?"

He hesitated before saying, "Stu and Ezra. But don't worry, I heard Stu's in a slump."

I ignored him and looked up at the scoreboard on the wall. Stu and Ezra had cleaned house against Zoe and Oliver in the first round. There was no way they could have earned such a decisive victory if either one of the players was in a slump. Great.

When Liberty announced the next two matches for the second round, one of those being ours, two spectators in particular began cheering. I looked toward the source.

Ruby and Sheriff Bloom sat on two golden stools that definitely didn't come from Sheehan's. The angel must have conjured them up herself. And who was going to correct *her* about standing room only?

But when I looked at the vocal pair, it became abundantly clear that they were not, in fact, cheering for Donovan and me.

"Traitor," I said to Ruby as I passed them.

She shrugged shamelessly. "I like to cheer for the winning team, that's all."

Bloom raised her glass of red wine, and Ruby clinked it with hers. The women burst into peals of laughter.

"Great to know the town is completely unprotected tonight," I said to Sheriff Bloom.

"Oh please, my presence here doesn't prevent me from doing my duty, should an emergency arise."

"No, but the wine might," Donovan said.

Bloom arched an eyebrow at him. "Looks like I'm being replaced as the town's most judgmental resident." She turned to Ruby. "Guess I can finally retire."

"And we can finally take that trip to Avalon we've been talking about for years." They burst into another fit of laughter, and I figured it was time for us to get a move on—it would do Donovan no good to keep mouthing off to the sheriff.

Stu and Donovan were matched up on one end of the table, and Ezra and I were on the other. I would have preferred to go against Stu just because I thought I could get in his head easier. He and I had worked so closely together that I knew a few buttons I could push to throw him off his game and give myself an opening.

But not Ezra. The South Wind was as much a mystery to me as he'd ever been. Pretty much all I knew about him was that he had stopped aging around 40 years ago, had once carried on with Ruby (and had recently taken it up again while the love spell covered the town), and he could sell fool's gold to a leprechaun for a premium price. None of that gave me an advantage as far as I could tell, but I tried it anyway.

Stu and Donovan tossed first, and Donovan gave us a narrow lead. Now it was my turn to not screw things up. Ezra tossed first, but not before I mentioned that I'd seen Ruby giving Count Malavic a sultry glance.

But the South Wind simply laughed. "Her and everyone else who thinks no one is watching." Then he slid a puck right into the center of the target.

Sphinx's riddle! So much for that.

I grabbed my puck and inhaled to steady myself. Donovan was staring down the board at me, his startlingly blue eyes intense and cutting.

... Could I see myself marrying him?

My toss looked promising for all of half a second before it went wide into the gutter.

Donovan cringed and said nothing, and I cursed under my breath.

Focus, Nora!

Why was I even thinking about marriage? It wasn't like I was set on it with Tanner when he was still around. I was just as unsure of it then.

Wasn't I?

Ezra had another incredible toss, and I glared at Landon through the crowd. This was his revenge, wasn't it? I beat him, so he gets in my head but acts like it's totally unintentional.

A North Wind *would* play that long game.

I shook the thought away. A North Wind *could* think

up that long game, but Landon wouldn't. This was all on me.

I focused and this toss was a little better. It scored us a point, which was nothing like the ten Ezra had already put up this round, but it was better than nothing.

When his next toss collided with his puck in the bullseye, causing both to explode and earning him ten more points, Donovan lost it. He threw his arms into the air and turned to Liberty. "There's no way! I've played against Ezra before and he's not this good."

Ezra shrugged. "I've been practicing."

"Practicing magic," Donovan snapped back.

For fang's sake, was this going to go to blows?

"Throw Stringfellow out!" Ruby barked.

I shot her a sharp look, and she sipped her wine.

"Hey," I said, stepping between Donovan and Liberty before he tried to pick a fight with a freaking genie. "Let it go. It was just a good shot." Donovan clenched his jaw, but did as I asked.

But by the final round, I was firmly in agreement with Donovan. There was just no way Ezra wasn't using magic. And if anyone had doubt about that, his fourth and final shot in the last round should have obliterated it. His puck was clearly headed for the gutter when the direction of its spin changed completely and it headed back for the middle of the table, landing a half inch from the innermost circle of the target.

Donovan was beside himself, gesturing wildly, pacing, and appealing to Liberty. But I still had one shot left. If I could somehow aim so that it exploded the closest one of Ezra's pucks at just the right angle, I could possibly set off a chain reaction through two of the other ones. That would erase just enough of his points that we would be tied and head into another round.

I lined it up, ignoring the distraction of Ruby's and Bloom's chants for "Team Stuzra" and Donovan's continued appeals, and focused. I could make this shot. Maybe not every time, but it was one I'd done before while practicing in Donovan's living room.

The puck slid down the table, crashed into the closest of Ezra's, causing a minor explosion, just as planned.

But that was it. The angle wasn't quite right, and the domino effect didn't come to pass. We'd lost.

It sucked, but I wasn't exactly heartbroken. At no point had I expected to make it to the finals, so it was only a matter of when we were eliminated.

As Donovan continued to beg and plead with Liberty that Stu and Ezra should be disqualified for breaking the magic rules, the winners approached me.

Stu Manchester nodded. "Good game, Ms. Ashcroft."

"Back atcha."

"Nah," said the deputy, "I played my worst game in a while."

I smiled and shrugged. "At least you got it out of your system."

Ezra said, "I thought you had it on that last one."

"It would have taken a real stroke of luck," I said. "Or magic."

"Ah," he said, "but we both know magic is against the rules." He winked.

I nodded. "And we both know you hate rules."

He chuckled but neither confirmed nor denied the

implication, and the two men left to thank their cheering section.

Donovan had stopped yelling at Liberty, which either meant the genie had lost patience and blinked him out of existence or Donovan had wandered off to use the restroom or get another drink. Either way, he hadn't even bothered to come tell me "good game" or reassure me that I didn't blow it. Maybe he was mad at me.

I decided I didn't care that much if he was. It would blow over. He was competitive, I already knew that from last year's Lunasa cook-off and, well, everything else he ever did. Being competitive wasn't a sin. Gaia knew I was competitive as all get out now and then.

I spotted Zoe and Oliver, who I hadn't yet said hello to tonight.

"For what it's worth," Oliver said as soon as he saw me, "I believe Ezra might have been using magic."

I waved him off. "It's fine. I don't care that much." I nodded at Zoe. "How's it going?"

As always, she grinned like I'd paid her a compliment just by acknowledging her. "Oh, great! I mean, we got out on the first round, but that was to be expected. I'm pretty terrible, and we were up against the Lytefoots. They've had hundreds of years to practice."

Oliver's eyes were glued to her as she spoke, like every word was a little gift just for him. He rubbed her back and said, "You did really well."

I bit back a grin that I knew would only embarrass him and said, "I think I'm almost ready for the next test."

Our tutoring arrangement had turned into distance learning as of late, and I think we were both fine with that. While Oliver wasn't the worst company, I don't think he felt the same about Ruby and me. Not that he didn't like us, just that Ruby didn't like to play by the rules, and I took every chance I could to get out of reading the textbooks and spell books he pushed on me. Our lessons were officially stressing him out, not to mention depriving him of quality Zoe time.

So we'd made arrangements with Mancer Academy to have Oliver simply test me each time I thought I'd mastered a section of content. How did we convince them of that? They never thought the Coven would sign off on it, and they were happy to pass the buck along. Unfortunately for the Academy, they weren't aware of extenuating circumstances: namely, that I hadn't gone straight to the *Eastwind Watch* with what I knew about High Priestess Springsong killing her predecessor, and that meant it was in her best interest to keep me happy in whatever small ways she could. The Coven signed off on the new educational structure quick, fast, and in a hurry.

Nothing like a little potential blackmail to grease the wheels of bureaucracy.

"What do you mean, the next test?" Oliver asked. "You still have to retake the last one."

"I thought we were skipping over the practical tests. You know I'm still terrible with a wand, and I'll probably always be."

He shifted uncomfortably. "I can't just pass you when you don't know how to perform basic spells."

"Yeah, you can. It's easy. No one will even know. And if anyone in the Coven finds out I couldn't blast my way out of a paper bag, I assume it'll only make their day. Maybe even their week."

Zoe was nodding along amicably with me, but Oliver

only looked even more uncomfortable, so I said, "You know what? Why are we even talking about this in a pub? Let's forget about it and pick it up again on Monday." That seemed to cheer him, and I stepped to the side to keep from blocking their view of the next matches.

I knocked into something solid and on instinct said, "Oh sorry," before seeing that it was Ansel Saxon I'd bumped into. He didn't even notice. He clutched a beer in his hand and glared at the table where his wife and sister were about to take on two leprechauns I didn't know.

Darius Pine stood on the other side of him. The two werebears had been eliminated in the last round, and they appeared to be having a good sulk about it.

"She must have been practicing without telling me," Ansel growled. "That's the only way they could have beaten us."

Darius just grunted.

"For a second there," Ansel continued, "I thought Sasha was going to throw the game just to get on your good side."

"Oh, shut it. No sister of yours would do that."

"If she would, it'd be for you."

"Why you don't give that a rest? That was years ago. We were both practically cubs."

Teasing Darius appeared to be putting Ansel in higher spirits, because he said, "Sure, and now you're full-grown bears. It could be fun. And now that she's back on the market again—"

"Don't be weird."

"What? I'd love to have you as a brother-in-law! You should take it as a compliment."

"I'm not going after your newly single sister, Ansel." Darius paused then added, "We both know I'd find a way to screw it up anyhow."

Poor Darius. He was practically cursed when it came to romance. The sleuth leader of Eastwind's werebears had the worst luck with women of anyone in Eastwind. Well, except maybe Stu. But Stu didn't try half as hard as Darius did in that arena. And Darius had looks going for him in a big way.

Donovan appeared with a fresh drink and I expected him to hand it to me, but instead he took a sip from it. "Good game," he said stiffly.

"You didn't get me one?" I nodded at his drink.

"Huh? Oh. I got you one earlier. I didn't know you wanted another."

I decided not to point out that I hadn't asked for one earlier either, but instead I just said, "It's fine. I have to use the ladies' room anyway."

* * *

There was a long break before the final match, during which Jane, now eliminated, located me in the crowd. As we had begun recapping some of the night's events, Sasha Fontaine hovered behind Jane, but didn't involve herself in the conversation. As Jane laughed about her husband's sulking, it occurred to me to wonder if Sasha was Greta's mother. Ansel had a couple of younger sisters, but if this was the mother of the young waitress at Medium Rare, the awkwardness made plenty of sense; Greta's mother had forced her to quit her job working for me during the worst tensions between witches and weres only half a year ago. While she'd since let her daughter return, I had no reason to believe she'd suddenly taken to witches.

Thankfully, Jane didn't give two licks about that. She chose her friends based on who she liked, not who people thought she should like.

But still, Sasha kept her body angled away from us, and when I asked her a question about the match to try to get her involved, she walked off.

"Sorry," Jane said. "Don't take it personally."

"Why not? It seems personal."

She scrunched up her nose. "Ah, yeah, well, I guess it is."

"That's Greta's mom, right?"

"Yep."

"Say no more."

Jane nodded. "She's not usually such a…"

"Snob?" I supplied.

"Yep. But don't think that's me defending her for her bigoted beliefs. If I've told her once, I've told her a thousand times that she needs to broaden her horizons. Woman doesn't listen."

Liberty announced that it was almost time for the final match, and half the crowd stampeded to the bar to get another drink.

Going against the crowd, I saw Donovan. This time he had two drinks and handed me one. "Sorry about last time."

Jane stuck her hand on her hip. "You didn't bring me one? Some gentleman."

He finished a long sip then said, "You had your chance for free drinks from me, and you turned them down."

"Fangs and claws, boy. The ink had hardly dried on my divorce papers, I was your supervisor, and you're a good ten years younger than me."

Now *this* was something I hadn't known about. I leaned back and indulged myself in this little bit of unexpected entertainment.

"Ten years is nothing," Donovan said. "It just means I have more stamina than the men your age."

"Not more than Ansel," she said.

He opened his mouth to reply then paused. "Yeah, that's probably true." Finally, he seemed to remember who I was and that he was dating me. "Oh, don't worry, this was a while ago."

"Not *that* long ago," I said. "Can't be more than a few years. But don't worry. If I have to come in second to anyone, I don't mind it being Jane."

"Oh please," he said, leaning close, "You became my first choice the second I laid eyes on you."

A tingle ran through my body as he wrapped an arm around my waist, leaning me back and kissing me.

"That's my cue to leave," Jane mumbled before she walked away.

Chapter Four

The final match was Stu and Ezra versus Ted and Count Malavic.

Everyone picked a side, and it was heavily weighted against the vampire and the grim reaper. Although I knew Ted to be one of the most harmless and lighthearted people in town, not everyone felt that way about him or had the opportunity to dispel their biases through forced interaction. And whatever forced interactions some of them *had* shared with him were not under the best of circumstances. So, despite his protests that he only cleaned up the bodies of the dead, many still assumed he had a little something to do with the selection of who stayed and who went.

I decided to root for him. Not for Malavic, though. No matter how much I liked Ted, I couldn't hope for anything good to come to Sebastian Malavic. That vampire had rubbed me wrong from day one, and while he'd proven himself useful on occasion, especially when big crawly things were pouring through the portal into the center of town, only a fool would actually like him. And I think he knew that and didn't mind it. He cared more for power than affection.

I also rooted for Ezra and Stu. Why not? Ezra had probably cheated, but I liked them both, and at least they'd come up and told me "good game" after the match, unlike some people...

Donovan was solidly anti-Stu and Ezra, though I wasn't sure he would be rooting for the other team.

I leaned over after he shouted yet another cheating accusation at Ezra and said, "Can you take it down a notch? At least if Stu and Ezra win, we can say we were eliminated by this year's champions."

It wasn't enough of an argument to completely turn his mood around, but it did keep him from continuing to yell once the play started.

The match was close and went into extra rounds, but ultimately the competition concluded with Ruby and Bloom cheering wildly, singing a chant whose words I couldn't make out, and Donovan erupting into outrage again before rushing at Liberty Freeman with a new set of allegations.

While most of the room went over to Stu and Ezra to celebrate, I approached Ted. "Good game."

"It was, wasn't it?"

"You don't sound sad," I said.

"Why would I be? We made it to the finals! Besides, look how happy everyone is."

I looked around. He wasn't wrong. "But they're happy that you lost."

He nodded, his dark reaper hood billowing around his head. "Exactly. The count and I have won for the last three years, but everyone loves to see a reigning champion knocked off his throne. So I was able to make them happy by losing."

"Wait... did you throw the game?"

"Oh, no, no, no. I would never do that. I suspect Ezra used magic to cheat!" And again, he didn't sound at all upset.

"So how come you're not over there, backing up my boyfriend?"

I nodded to where Donovan was pacing in front of Liberty, who looked about three seconds away from officially being done with Donovan's nonsense.

Ted followed my gaze. "Oh, good. Looks like Malavic is going to intervene."

"What?" I saw the count heading toward them. No, that was not good. The only thing that could make this situation worse for Donovan was getting the vampire involved. "I'd better go."

Malavic was holding Donovan back while Liberty turned and joined the rest of the celebration. He grinned at me when I arrived next to them. "Ah, I was wondering when his babysitter would show up."

"He's just a little drunk," I explained, hoping that was actually what was causing this totally ridiculous behavior. I didn't mind making a scene at a bar every so often, but this was something else. This was the kind of thing that might become part of scufflepuck folklore around Sheehan's.

"I'm just saying," Donovan protested, "there ought to be a rematch. Everyone saw the way his puck changed directions."

Malavic handed off Donovan's arm to me, passing the

torch of responsibility as he said, "There are no redos. Not in the game, not in real life." And now he looked at me. "Sometimes there are second chances, though. But only for those willing to risk it."

I shook my head and rolled my eyes. "I don't even know what you're saying, and I'm too tired to play your dumb games."

He smiled that cracked-earth grin of his, and said to Donovan, "Thank you for defending my honor. You're a real hero." And then he turned around and slipped off.

It wasn't long after that Fiona and Kelley reached their limit on the rowdiness and kicked everyone out a half-hour before closing time. A few witches had ridden brooms to the event, and the sheriff made quick work of vanishing those to avoid any drunken flying accidents. As their owners complained, she informed them they could pick up their rides at the sheriff's department the following day.

The crowd lingered in front of the pub for a while, but I was more than ready to go home and get in bed. Medium Rare was set to open late the next day, but I thought it might be nice to have a slow, easy morning. And I really did need to catch up on some studying if I was ever going to officially graduate.

The throng dissipated quickly once it reached the street, many of the folks splitting off toward their homes in Erin Park and the surrounding neighborhoods while the rest of us made toward the center of town. Donovan walked next to me, and I allowed him to hold my hand, even though I wasn't super thrilled about the way he'd conducted himself. Ezra carried Ruby down the street in his arms, and Stu recapped each of his throws, play by play, to Stella and Kayleigh Lytefoot.

Our group of twenty or so began to thin, but by the time we were almost to Fulcrum Park, there were still easily a dozen among us.

I don't know who saw the body first, but a chill ran down my spine the second I heard the bloodcurdling scream.

Chapter Five

"Back up! Everyone take a step back!" Stu hollered at the gawking group.

Nobody listened, so he simply muscled his way through to get a look.

I was already there, having known the second I heard the scream what must have happened.

I stared down at the man's body. It just looked like he'd passed out or fallen asleep on his stomach in the grass. "Who is it?" I asked Stu. I didn't even know what kind of being we were looking at—were, witch, something else?

I could rule out faun and minotaur since there were no animal parts, and fairy and pixie since there were no wings. He was certainly pale enough that he could have been an elf or vampire, but I suspected neither of those were what we were dealing with.

Stu checked for a pulse to confirm what was obvious to the rest of us, and then he rolled the body over onto its back.

"Twenty tines," he cursed. "It's Dmitri."

I'd heard that name before tonight, but when?

Then it clicked.

"Dmitri as in the witch?"

Stu nodded. "Dmitri Flint." He turned back toward the onlookers, still crouching. "You folks go on and get home. You're all drunk and no help to begin with. Show the man some respect."

"You're drunk, too," came a deep voice from the small crowd.

"Yeah, but I hold it better!" the deputy shouted. "Now get a move on!"

I raised to standing and he said, "Not you, Ms. Ashcroft. I might need you to stick around."

I groaned. Did this long night really have to get longer? "Maybe Ruby can—"

"Ruby can do no such thing!" Ruby announced. "Ruby is too old for swirls like this anymore. Besides, Ruby is retired!"

Ezra, still carrying her, said, "Ezra will escort her home."

I shot him a sharp look. "Ezra will make sure she's safe inside and then depart."

"Ruby is a grown woman and can make her own decisions!" said Ruby. She reached behind him, smacking him on the backside and said, "Onward, my steed!"

Ezra tossed me what-can-you-do? shrug and continued carrying her down the hill toward our house, the pair of them loudly singing a lilting tune.

Once the rest of the group, except for Donovan, had cleared out, Stu asked, "You sense anything? You reckon it's murder or natural causes?"

"I don't sense much of anything," I said, "but I've been drinking all night. Doesn't exactly help the Insight."

He nodded. "I don't see anything that immediately points to homicide, but do me a favor and let me know as soon as possible if he turns up." He sighed and slapped a palm to his forehead, shaking his head slowly. "A dead guy in the middle of the road. Can't I just get one day off without anything terrible happening?"

"Maybe you should call for Bloom."

"Yeah, I suppose I should. Well, you two kids get home and try to get some shut-eye. I know the sight of this isn't conducive to a full-night's sleep, but well, nothing you can do about that."

"We'll be fine, Stu," Donovan assured him. But I could still hear a little iciness in his tone.

"You take care of yourself," I said to the deputy. No one in Eastwind needed a vacation like Stu Manchester needed a vacation.

Donovan put his arm around me, and we proceeded on down the road. But when we got to the place where he would have gone left and I would have gone right, he seemed just fine continuing to the right along with me.

I pulled up short. To say I wasn't feeling it after his behavior and finding a body in the middle of the road would be a gross understatement. But I knew he didn't handle rejection well, so I eased in. "I think I just need some sleep tonight."

"Yeah, that's fine. I'm tired too." He tried to continue forward with me, but I didn't follow, so he stopped walking again.

"I sleep better when I'm not sharing a bed," I said.

His lips parted slightly as the not-so-subtle hint landed. "Is this because of the tournament?"

"You mean how you spent most of the night verbally abusing a genie until a vampire had to intervene? No, it's not about that."

He narrowed his eyes. "Ah, I see. I embarrassed you."

"Yeah, a little. But it's really not about that," I said. Because it wasn't *entirely* about that.

"What's it about?"

I remembered Landon showing me the gleaming sapphire. "I'm tired, that's all. Too much socializing. I just want to be alone for a little bit to recharge before work tomorrow."

He frowned, but, thankfully, bought it. "Yeah, okay. I get that. There *were* a lot of people there tonight." He closed the space between us and pulled me close. "I'm sorry I got too competitive and embarrassed you. I know I can be a little much."

I felt myself soften against him. "It's okay. Everyone was drinking."

"I'll apologize to Liberty in the morning. Well, maybe not the morning. I plan on sleeping off a hangover until about noon. But I'll send him a letter before I go into Franco's tomorrow."

I smiled and he kissed me. "If that dead guy shows up in your bedroom, do me a favor."

"What's that?" I asked.

"Let him know you have a jealous boyfriend who'll kick his hide if he lays a hand on you, and that being dead already isn't going to save him."

I laughed. "I'll be sure to pass along the word. But hopefully it'll be a quiet night."

One last (long) kiss, and we parted ways.

When I finally made it inside, I expected Grim and Monster to have made their way upstairs for the night, but instead, I found the munchkin cat hot on Grim's tail as he fled in circles around the parlor table, shouting, *"It was just a joke! I would never eat your food!"*

"We both know that's a lie," I replied, leaping out of the way as Grim tried to use me as a human shield. "Monster, it's too late for this. It's been a long night and I just want to go to sleep."

"If you think we're the loudest thing happening in the house tonight..."

He didn't have to spell it out. I groaned and said, "Everybody upstairs."

Clifford was sleeping outside Ruby's bedroom door on the second story landing when I beat on her door and said, "Sound silencing spell, please."

Clifford wagged his tail, which I took to mean "thank you."

I climbed up the stairwell to my room on the third story, kicked off my boots, flopped facedown into bed, and was out like a Quenched light.

Until...

It was the humidity that did it. Or maybe it was Grim's weight pressing down the mattress, so I rolled slowly into his fuzzy legs. Either way, when I woke up, the first thing I saw was his slobbery jowls hanging open over me as his hot breath assaulted my face in repeat blasts. "Off the bed," I mumbled, trying to get my bearings.

"I can't sleep."

I opened and closed my eyes a few times, struggling to follow along. *"What, did you have a nightmare?"*

"Unfortunately, not. I love nightmares. It's the tapping that's keeping me awake."

"What tapping?" But then the sound rose to the forefront of my brain.

"At the window," he said.

I whipped my head around to see. "Oh, for fang's sake." I temporarily collapsed back onto the bed before rallying and going to the window. I cracked it open just enough so that the spirit could hear me clearly. "Come on in."

I closed the window tight again, and the ghost of Dmitri Flint nodded and glided through the glass. Now that I wasn't trying not to gawk (like I had been back at the park), I could get a real look at him. His dark hair was long and curly, and he wore it with the sides pulled back into a knot. Though I guessed him at a handful of years older than me, he had the large round eyes of a dangerously curious boy. There was likely a good story behind his visibly crooked nose, and laugh lines framing his mouth completed the impression that he had, in fact, lived every day with vigor like it might be his last.

"Sorry," he said, "I didn't want to intrude. I mean, more than I am."

Offering him the empty chair in the corner of the room, I went and took a seat on the end of my bed and tried to will my eyes to stay open. "You're here and I'm awake, so we might as well get into it."

As Dmitri floated past her, Monster woke up with a start, looked around in all directions, then arched her back and bounded away from the source of the chill. She could always sense the spirits coming in and out, but since she couldn't see them like Grim and I could, they sometimes sent the usually fierce feline into a panic when they snuck up on her.

Once she was tucked under the bed (Grim followed her for good measure, flattening himself out as much as he could to shimmy underneath), I went ahead and launched into it. "I presume you were murdered."

But to my surprise, Dmitri frowned and shook his head slowly. "No, not murdered."

I squinted at him through the darkness. The moon was low in the sky, giving off little light, which allowed him to glow unusually bright. "You sure?"

"Pretty sure."

"O-kay... Unfinished business then?"

"No, none that I can think of."

I blinked. "All right, then you haven't come to terms with your own mortality. That has to be why you're here."

"Again, sorry, but no. I came to terms with that years ago."

I was stumped. "Then why are you here?"

He chuckled. "That's what I came to see you about. I have—*had*—a preexisting heart condition that I knew could kill me at the drop of a coin. Doctor discovered it a few years back but couldn't explain it. I even traveled to a specialist in Avalon and she couldn't figure it out. So I made peace with the fact that every day could be my last, and I got all my affairs in order. And then I just kept on living. Until I didn't."

"Clearly," I said. I mulled over the few facts I had, then asked, "You're sure you weren't murdered?"

"Pretty sure. The specialist told me it would be a fairly painless death, just feel like someone punched me in the chest, and then I might feel some sharp pains in my heart and then it'd be over. Well, that's about what I felt. And I don't know of anyone who would want me dead."

I waved that off. "The murdered rarely do. What were you doing when it happened?"

"Just walking up the hill toward Sheehan's for the tournament." He paused. "Oh man, Bryant must be furious at me. He was so set on winning this year."

"I'm sure he'll understand when he hears the news."

"Then you've underestimated how competitive he can be. He won't accept my death as a valid excuse for not making it."

He was right. I'd underestimated Bryant. Again, I was reminded of how little I actually knew about him. I considered suggesting to Donovan that he and Bryant team up for next year's tournament. But then I quickly dismissed it; pairing up two people that competitive would likely turn into a nightmare for everyone.

Dmitri continued. "I assume it was the hill that did it. I'm not as in shape as I used to be, and the strain might have triggered the heart defect."

I nodded. "I'm not a doctor, but that seems plausible enough." It wasn't an especially steep hill going toward Erin Park, and Dmitri wasn't what I would call overweight, but what did I know about how all that worked? I was a psychic who owned a restaurant, not a cardiologist.

But still, I lacked even a hunch about why he was sitting in my bedroom chatting with me rather than enjoying the great beyond.

38

A couple things were clear, though. First, this would take some looking into; and, second, I was too tired to start now. "Can you do me a favor?"

"Sure. I got nothing but time."

"Great. Can you come back tomorrow morning?"

"Of course. Unless, you know, I move on. In which case—"

"Problem solved."

"Yep." He grinned, and I was slightly annoyed to realize that I liked him. It was always a shame when I met someone I enjoyed only after they were dead. Of course, that happened very rarely—most people weren't made *less* obnoxious by death.

Which left me even more puzzled about why Dmitri hadn't moved on.

He let himself out through the window just as his visible form dissipated from sight, and I crawled back under the covers.

Sleep should have come easy. But it didn't.

Because while nothing about this felt like an emergency, it was just strange enough to leave me unsettled. And what was unsettling by Eastwind standards could be downright deadly.

Chapter Six

Sunday morning came too soon. Far, far, too soon. But at least my decision to wait until 8 a.m. to open Medium Rare, rather than the usual 6 a.m. time I'd settled on since transitioning away from the 24-hour schedule, allowed me just a little more time to lie in bed before dragging myself out.

Ruby was already at the stove when I wandered down in an oversized T-shirt that went down to my knees. She had a cup of tea in hand as she flipped slices of bacon on the griddle.

"That smells amazing."

She glanced over her shoulder and smiled at me. "I made enough to share."

She brought the kettle over to the table, along with a cup of tea that was already steeping. A delightful floral aroma with a hint of citrus rose up from the cup, welcoming me to a new day. A delicious warmth spread through me at the mere scent of it.

"Can I help with anything?" I asked.

"No. I have it all under control. Have a seat. You look like you had a rough night."

"And you look like you shed ten years."

She chuckled. "Only ten? It feels like more than that."

I waited until the bacon was already on the table and she'd had a seat and poured herself a fresh cup before I decided to break news to her that would undoubtedly sour her mood.

Scooping half a dozen pieces of bacon onto my plate (there were easily two dozen she'd cooked up to cover the two witches and three familiars), I said, "So, I had a visitor last night."

She simply arched an eyebrow lazily and nibbled her bacon. "Not of the same variety as mine, I presume?"

"No. Definitely not that."

"Too bad."

"Indeed." I cleared my throat. "Dmitri came by."

"Hm," she said. "Murder then?"

"Well, no."

As if summoned, he appeared in the parlor over by the fire, which blazed blue to keep the place nice and cool as the summer sun was already rising in the sky. He took in his surroundings, his eyes sticking for a minute on the threatening assortment of clutter hanging from her ceiling.

"Don't worry," she said, "I won't banish you so long as you don't try to possess anyone."

I nodded for him to approach, and he did.

Once I'd explained the strange situation to Ruby,

with Dmitri filling in details as she asked for them, she fell into a thoughtful silence and cupped her tea in both hands. Then, finally, she turned to Dmitri and said, "I can conclusively say I don't know why you're here." She grabbed another piece of crunchy bacon and chomped into it. "I would have to look into it further. Of course"—and she addressed this directly to me—"I'm retired, so I won't do that." And now she smiled at Dmitri. "But lucky for you, Nora is not. And she has a not-entirely-unimpressive track record with solving this sort of thing."

Okay, no help from Ruby. Noted. "Where would you start... if you weren't retired?"

"The same place I would always start. Talk with the people who knew him best. They should be most familiar with his faults, and if you can convince them to speak ill of the dead, you might actually learn something useful."

"And if I can't get them to speak ill of the dead?"

She shrugged. "Check in with Stu. See if he's found any signs of foul play."

"So you think it's murder?"

"I don't think anything anymore except that I ought to take a trip to the library today to pick up a few new reads. I just finished *Eat, Prey, Stalk* and it was quite the thriller! I'm hoping to find something else in a similar vein. Nothing like an exciting read during a lazy summer!" She stood and carried her plate into the kitchen. "You know, I've always suspected that I would like retirement, but I never knew it would be quite so wonderful. It's like I've died and gone to Heaven, except without the hassle of death or the judgment and bureaucracy of a flock of angels."

I turned to Dmitri and fed him the line I'd had to say way more times than I'd like to admit since coming to Eastwind: "Let me put on some pants, then we'll look into your death."

Chapter Seven

Bryant was the obvious first choice of friend to speak with. Not only were he and Dmitri close, but he also worked at Medium Rare. Let's hear it for convenience when I haven't quite kicked my hangover!

But Bryant wasn't scheduled to come in until later that afternoon, so Dmitri agreed to wait patiently until that time came. Like he'd said, he had no pressing matters and nothing but time.

I discovered two important things during that shift. First, I was officially past the age where I could have more than two drinks in a night and not get a hangover. Knowing that about oneself should not be dismissed as trivial.

And second, Dmitri was great company. When two weres argued that they'd never received their omelets—after I'd personally delivered them—Dmitri had said, "Looks like you have a couple of eggheads on your hands," which admittedly a stupid joke but also

44

exactly what I'd needed to hear to go from the verge of being officially annoyed to biting back a smile.

And when a little group of Coven witches came in, so tightly wrapped in their own gossip that I could hardly take their order without them acting put out by the interruption, he fed me bits and pieces of gossip about *them* that really took the edge off their air of moral superiority.

But the biggest surprise of the morning happened after he'd spent two hours in the corner booth, chatting it up with Ted and Grim. As the reaper slipped the hellhound small bites of various breakfast meats, it became obvious that Dmitri had won the favor of my familiar. Or if he hadn't, he was dangerously close. How he managed to do that without being able to physically toss the hound food was beyond me.

I was hoping Stu would make his usual visit, but I wasn't surprised when he didn't. Between the alcohol consumption and the dead body, if the deputy had even been relieved from his shift yet, he would likely go straight home to sleep.

Bryant was almost an hour late for his shift, and, boy, did he look terrible. I would have been mad, but I couldn't easily forget that one of his closest friends had died the night before. The fact that he hadn't simply called in sick was admirable enough, and I let the tardiness slide without comment.

"You sure you're good to work?" I asked as he tied on his apron.

"What else is there to do?"

"Mope? Sleep?"

He blinked. "Oh yeah. I guess that sounds way better

than working." He sighed, spreading his arms. "Well, I'm here."

"Great. Before you get started, I need to talk to you."

"I know, I'm sorry. I should have let you know I'd be running late. But I totally lost track of time, and it was all I could do to—"

"No, no. It's not that. It's... something else."

He squinted his swollen eyes at me for a moment before his mouth fell open. "He visited you?"

"Let's talk out back." I leaned to the side to see around him and waved to Ted. The reaper perked up and I pointed to Dmitri. Ted nodded and got the spirit's attention, directing it my way. I waved him over and a moment later the three of us were standing in the hot afternoon sun behind the diner. I could hardly see Dmitri in this bright of light, but I could hear him just fine.

"Tell him his tail's looking great today." Dmitri smiled mischievously.

I was not telling him that.

Bryant stared at me unblinkingly through glassy eyes. "So, he was murdered?"

"Not as far as I can tell."

Dmitri piped up again. "Seriously, tell him his tail's looking exceptional today. Extra fluffy."

I continued to ignore him as Bryant asked, "Then why did he visit you?"

"It's possible," said the spirit, "that the reason I'm stuck here is that I need to tell Bryant, one last time, that his tail looks amazing."

Again, ignoring the spirit, I said, "I'm not sure. Something is keeping him here."

Bryant hitched a silver eyebrow. "Unfinished business?"

Dmitri was yelling now. "Yes! I need him to know that his tail—"

I balled my hands into fists until my nails dug in, and ground out, "He wants you to know your tail looks... good today."

For a split second, Bryant looked at me like I might be insane. And that was fine. I pretty much lived my life in a state of questioning my own sanity, so I totally understood where he was coming from.

But then his eyes narrowed, and he hissed, "Is that son of a banshee with us right now?" And before I could answer, he began whirling around, searching futilely in all directions and shouting, "If you tell her that story, I'll make sure you never rest in peace!"

Oh, now I was intrigued.

As Dmitri howled with laughter at his friend, I couldn't help but inquire, "What story?"

Bryant stopped in his tracks and said, "No, not a chance, Nora. It's just this thing that happened at Sheehan's a long time ago and..." He shook his head. "Not important. Maybe his unfinished business is that his stupid hide left me hanging at the scufflepuck tournament last night."

Dmitri was still chuckling as he said, "Doubt that's it. I don't care much about scufflepuck."

"I don't have to tell him for you," I reminded Bryant, "he can hear just fine. You just can't hear or see him."

Bryant nodded. "Right, right... So, wait, I can say anything I want to him right now, and he just has to sit and listen? He can't argue back?"

I saw where this was going. "Yeah, but that's really not why I'm—"

"Hey, Dmitri, guess what? I thought your vegetable stew sucked! I always hated it. Who makes stew and doesn't add meat?"

Dmitri met my eyes. "I wasn't a fan of it either. I just loved watching him pretend to like it."

"And it needed more salt!" Bryant continued angrily, and I reminded myself that people mourned in strange ways. "And a little rosemary wouldn't kill you! That stuff grows like weeds around here. Not hard to get ahold of it."

While this all seemed very cathartic for him, he did need to get back to work and before he did that, I had some important questions I wanted answered.

But I let him go on for a little while longer at the behest of Dmitri who explained it would be good for the werewolf to let it all out.

And let it all out, he did.

Minutes later, after Bryant had admitted that he *hadn't* ever paid Dmitri back for his share of the party they'd thrown together eight years ago and he'd only said he had because he knew Dmitri wouldn't have kept track, I stepped in. "Feel better?"

Bryant looked exhausted. "Yeah, I guess so."

"Usually people want to tell the ghosts of their loved ones that they'll miss them and won't forget them, but I guess airing all your dirty laundry is fine. Everyone grieves differently. Regardless, I do have some questions for you."

His face drooped when I said it. "Oh... yeah. I guess I shouldn't have just come clean like that before murder's been ruled out. Might make me look kind of... suspicious."

"Maybe, but for what it's worth, I don't think you killed Dmitri. He didn't share this with you, but he had a heart condition that was basically a ticking clock. I mean, more than hearts already are."

Bryant tilted his head to the side. "He did? Why didn't he tell me this?"

"I didn't want you to worry about it, you idiot," Dmitri said.

"He didn't want to worry you. There was no point in worrying because the doctors said there was nothing he could do about it. They didn't really know what was causing it, only that it could take him at any moment—in two days or twenty years."

Bryant massaged the back of his neck. "Yeah, I guess that could be said of anyone, though. You never know when it's your time."

"Too true," I replied. "The point is, I'm *pretty* sure it was his time, but not totally sure. I want to rule out the possibility of murder, so I need you to tell me anything you know about him that might have made someone want to kill him."

"You mean, outside of all the stuff I just said?" he asked sheepishly.

"Yeah, outside of that, which all seemed pretty minor anyway."

"People have murdered for less."

"Don't I know it."

Bryant considered the question for a moment, and then replied, "No, I just don't see why anyone would. You'd have to ask him."

"I have. He doesn't know either. What about unfinished business?"

"What about it?"

"You know of any he might have overlooked or... withheld?"

Dmitri crossed his translucent arms over his chest. "I don't appreciate the lack of trust."

But Bryant just shook his head. "Nothing I know about outside of the unfinished business we all have at any given point in time. He might have some unpaid bills, or maybe he wants to see some woman again, or he doesn't want to move on from eating Franco's Pizza's beef lasagna twice a week."

I nodded. "I can sympathize with that one."

"Right. So can everyone who's eaten that stuff. But I'm sure there are other people who've died in Eastwind recently and didn't linger to have another bite."

I sighed. "Agreed. Well, you'd better get back to work, but if you think of anything else, let me know."

He nodded but didn't immediately make for the door. "One last thing," he said hesitantly. "Seeing as how this might be my last chance to talk with Dmitri, even indirectly..."

"Yes?"

"Would you ask him if I can have his Zatrian drums?"

I didn't bother reminding him that Dmitri could hear him just fine. It was a tough concept for people to remember; it went against their natural instincts for communication to be one-way like this.

Dmitri replied and I relayed the message. "He says of course but you'd better get in there and take the drums before they start looking over the will. Spare key to his house is nestled in the crook of the fig tree in his backyard."

"Great! I've always wanted a pair of Zatrians. Okay, back to work. Tell Dmitri..." but then he remembered and stared into the space where I'd just addressed the spirit. "I'll miss you, buddy. Hope you move on soon. And thanks for the drums."

Chapter Eight

The great thing about this case was the lack of urgency. It was rare that I had time to think about the full scope without the ghost in question badgering me.

I was pretty sure there was no foul play involved in this one, and Dmitri had a good head on him about the irrelevance of time in his current predicament, so whenever he could wrap it up and carry onto the next place worked for him. A day, a week, a month... I could tell it didn't matter that much to him.

And having a ghost to keep me entertained, rather than one who seemed bent on driving me to an early grave, was a pleasant deviation from the norm.

As usual, I had a good idea of the next move to make (Ruby had laid it out pretty clearly, anyhow) but I felt no need to hurry from one location to the next, working up an unnecessary sweat in the process.

Regardless, it wasn't prudent to not take *any* action on his behalf, so after my shift on Monday, Dmitri, Grim, and I made for the sheriff's department to meet up with Stu and get an update.

I was playing translator between Grim and Dmitri as we strolled out of the Outskirts and toward the station (this time it was Dmitri who couldn't hear the other party and not the other way around). After Grim's story of his most recent weekend getaway to the Deadwoods concluded, Dmitri said, "I do wish I'd have gone there. It just always seemed so dangerous. In hindsight, even if something had killed me out there, I wouldn't have lost much time."

"It's not as fun as Grim makes it out to be," I said.

His eyes popped open wide. "You've been in the Deadwoods?"

"Yep. A couple of times, unfortunately."

"And?"

"You won't see me planning a camping trip out there."

"Wait a second," said Grim. *"If he's already dead..."*

I saw where my familiar was going with that. "You're right, Grim. He would fit right in."

"What's that?" said Dmitri.

"Grim was just pointing out that, now that you're dead and not in a hurry to move on, you could go see the Deadwoods without worrying."

Were there things in the Deadwoods that could harm a spirit? It wasn't impossible. But I decided not to mention it, because the look of excitement on Dmitri's face was too gratifying.

He bobbed as he floated beside me. "Great point! Ted invited me out to his cabin if I got bored. I think I'll have to take him up on it. What do you say, Grim?"

Grim wagged his tail and nodded his big, shaggy head.

"It's settled then! We'll start planning as soon as we wrap things up with the deputy."

Did I feel just a little left out?

Maybe. But not enough to make me want to venture into the Deadwoods for fun.

"Ask him if he wants to go as far as the Murderswamp. I haven't been there in ages! It's so deadly. So, so deadly..."

Once I mentioned the Murderswamp to Dmitri, that was all he wanted to talk about for the rest of the walk. It was a huge relief when I got to drop my translator duties and enter the cool air of the station.

Jingo the goblin looked up from the reception desk and straight-up rolled his eyes. Yes, he loved me. But even more than that, he loved Grim.

"If that hound even so much as raises a hind leg within twenty feet of my desk..."

"Don't worry," I assured him. "It was just that one time."

"I couldn't get the stink out. What do you even feed him?"

"Bacon and sausage, mostly."

"I would have guessed asparagus." He gave Grim one last glare then said, "Go on back. He's expecting you."

Stu's regularly austere desk was starting to look more and more like Sheriff Bloom's, and he didn't immediately glance up from the reports in front of him when we entered.

"Have a seat, Ms. Ashcroft."

I did, and we waited for a moment more before he set

down his pen, rubbed a hand over his bristly mustache, and said, "You heard anything from him?"

"Sure have. He's with me right now."

Stu sat up straighter. "No lie?"

"I'd never lie to you, Stu."

"Well? What's he got to say?"

And so I filled in the deputy with everything I knew about the situation, stopping short of mentioning where Dmitri hid his spare key—I'd tell Stu later if he asked, but I wanted to give Bryant an adequate head start at getting those drums before the place was locked down.

"Huh. Well, I suppose we'll hear back about the heart thing soon. Medical Examiner Stern is scheduled to complete her report tomorrow, and then it'll be a day or two before Magical Examiner Brightburn gets to take his turn."

"That's fine. There's no hurry."

"You're assuming," said Stu, "that he wasn't murdered. If he was murdered, this could simply be the first in a string of murders, in which case, there *is* a hurry."

While that possibility existed, I couldn't help but suspect his supposition had less to do with the specifics of the case and everything to do with the fact that Stu Manchester needed to take a holiday.

A small knock on the door, and then I heard Sheriff Bloom's voice behind me. "Oh, hello, Nora. I hope I'm not interrupting. I didn't realize anyone was here."

"Nope, not interrupting," I said. "I think we were just finishing up."

She smiled blandly as her eyes completed a quick scan of the room.

"Did you need something, Sheriff?" Stu asked.

"Yes, but it can wait. Nora, may I have a word with you?"

Her precise tone made me feel like I was being called into the principal's office.

As I stood, she added. "Alone."

When her eyes did another suspicious scan of the space, I knew she wasn't just talking about Grim and Stu.

"I'll just hang out here, then," Dmitri said.

"Good choice," I mumbled before following the angel out of Stu's office.

She brought me into hers and shut the door behind me. "I sensed a presence. Am I correct in assuming it is Dmitri Flint?"

"You are."

She nodded. "That's interesting. And does he believe he's been murdered?"

"No."

She nodded again. "I've met Dmitri a few times, and he's a congenial fellow. Quite likable."

"Yeah, it's a pleasant surprise."

"Would you like to know the capacity in which I've had interactions with him?" Her rigid posture and clipped tone were all the hints I needed.

"Oh. I'm guessing an official one."

"Yes. There are nearly two thousand people in this town, and most of them are born, grow up, and die of natural causes before I ever have occasion to learn their name. But I know his. He has involvement."

I felt like someone had smacked me on the back of the head. "He didn't mention anything about that." She was gracious enough to give me space to add, "Of course he didn't."

She adjusted her giant white wings and took a seat behind her paper fortress of a desk. "Before you came to town, I had many opportunities to work intimately with Ruby True on cases."

"She's told me about a few."

Bloom grinned. "I bet she has. But in working closely with her, I've learned that ghosts and living suspects aren't all that different. You can't trust them to say anything that would make themselves look bad. More than that, you can't expect them to be aware of all the people who might want to do them harm. If mortals had that ability, there would be a lot fewer murders because people could fortify their defenses more effectively.

"What I'm saying is that I don't think you should take Dmitri at his word, no matter how charismatic and honest he seems. It's not necessarily that he's intentionally obfuscating, just that we often can't trust our own mind to show us the relevant information about ourselves.

"Ruby once told me about a man named Sigmund Freud..."

"Please, Sheriff, if we're going to start talking about my parents, I'm going to need to sit down."

"No, it's not that. But you're welcome to have a seat anyway." I decided to remain standing, and she shrugged. "The part of his theories to which you refer does sound a bit like swirls to me. It's the part about 'superego' that I think about every day." She leaned back against her desk, sending a teetering stack of paperwork falling to the floor and not giving it an iota of attention. "The superego is quite the fraud, isn't it? It tells us that it only has our best interests in mind, that it knows right from wrong, and that when it tells us to do something, it's protecting us or driving us to be better. But there's only one thing the superego truly cares about, and that's protecting the reputation of the superego."

"No offense, Sheriff, but I don't follow why you're telling me this."

"Because it's crucial that law enforcement understand it, and whether you like it or not, that's one of the hats you wear in this town. Just because someone means to tell you the truth doesn't mean they will. Nearly everyone wants to believe they are a good person, even the career criminals. Their superego will do whatever twisting of facts necessary to preserve their positive self-image. If the bit of information you need from them might disrupt the story they tell themselves about their own goodness, then you cannot expect to hear it, no matter how honest they intend to be. The superego will hide that hard truth behind layers upon layers of excuses and justifications and identity until it would take a miracle to get to it."

I knew on almost an instinctive level that she was correct. How many times had my mind—or superego or whatever—supplied me with a convenient justification to do what I wanted with righteous moral imperative... only for me to realize later, and with some discomfort, that I was just doing what I wanted to do, *regardless* of what was right?

Now I did sit down, feeling strangely exhausted all of a sudden. "You don't believe I should trust Dmitri."

"No. I don't. But I don't think you, or anyone, should trust many people. At least not at their word. I suppose that suspicion comes with being able to detect guilt stains on the soul like I can. Everyone's a little guilty about something. And it's no coincidence that the people with the most active superegos carry around the most guilt; they won't let themselves admit to their mistakes and failings and imperfections long enough to do what it takes to purge the guilt by making things right."

"When you say Dmitri has involvement, what do you mean precisely?"

She steepled her fingers, touching the tips to her mouth before speaking. "I think you would do better to talk to those involved. The story they provide the sheriff right after the fact, when the superego is most energized regarding the incident, will be much different from the story they'll give to a Fifth Wind years later."

"You think people will be more upfront? More honest?"

Bloom chuckled. "As honest as they can be, like I said."

"Right."

"But that's not why I suggest it. People don't commit murder based on facts or reality; they commit murder based on the stories they believe to be true. The story may be one of 'the right thing to do' or 'it's them or me' or something more elaborate, but there's a story behind it nonetheless." She paused, leaning back in her wooden chair. "What stories people told themselves about Dmitri years ago are irrelevant; he wasn't murdered years ago. It's the stories those same people tell themselves about him today that will inform your opinion of whether murder seemed like a good and righteous option to them two days ago."

"And who do you think I should talk to?"

"To start, Greggory O'Leary. A leprechaun up in Erin Park and an old friend and accomplice of Dmitri. I'm sure he'll have a wealth of information for you if you can only get at it. And then, of course, the ever-delightful Count Sebastian Malavic."

"For fang's sake..."

"I agree. I don't envy you."

Oh well. What was an investigation if Malavic wasn't somehow involved? It would hardly even count. (No pun intended.)

"How deep am I getting here by following up on these leads?" I asked.

The angel took a moment to consider it. "I don't know. All I know is that during the last few interactions I've had with Dmitri Flint, there's been *something* there. A guilt that's not nebulous like most people's, but hard and dense like a stone. I don't know what it is, but I know it's not nothing."

Fantastic. More mysterious circumstances surrounding this. Why couldn't anything just be cut and dried? "You think it has something to do with his death?"

"My gut says yes," the angel replied. "What does your Insight say?"

Swirls. "Yes. It says yes, now that I know all this about him."

She rose, so I did too. She approached then placed a hand on my shoulder. I remembered the time she'd hugged me at the Lunasa Festival and how good that had felt. This was nothing like it, but it was definitely comforting. "You don't have to think the worst of him. On the scale of criminals in this town, he rates very low from what I know. I just don't want you going in blindly. I know that when you have the facts and fair warning, things turn out well for you. That's all this is."

I swallowed. "Thanks, Sheriff."

Her hand dropped from my shoulder and I took that as my cue.

And as I left her office, I thought, *Of course. The first ghost who visits me who I actually like, and he's hiding important things from me.*

Ah, well, just another day on the job that would no doubt be the death of me.

Chapter Nine

Grim and Dmitri followed me down the steps away from the Sheriff's Department. It was nearly dinner time (or so growled my stomach), but the late-spring sun was taking its sweet time setting, and the world was still bright.

"What'd she say?" Dmitri asked. "Are you in trouble? Did she get mad at you? Oh! Were you fined?"

I waited until we had a fair amount of distance from the station and said, "You need to tell me about your arrests. All of them." I didn't mean to sound so bitter, but I wasn't thrilled with him. His lack of disclosure had made me look like a bit of a fool in front of the Sheriff, and if there was anyone in this town whose approval I wanted more, I couldn't think of them.

"You haven't exactly been forthcoming, have you?" I said.

"What do you mean? About what?"

"Your criminal record."

"I wouldn't call it that. I've been slapped on the wrist a couple of times, spent one night in jail for drunken disorder. What can I say? I used to live it up. But finding out about my heart problem was the wake-up call I needed. I don't mess around with that stuff anymore."

"What stuff?"

"Stupid and reckless stuff."

"With Greggory O'Leary? Or Count Malavic?"

That caused him to pause, and he turned to look at me. "What did she say about them?"

"Only that they were part of your criminal record."

"I'm telling you, it's not a criminal record. I mean, sure, it *technically* is. But that also makes it sound so bad. It's more like mischief."

"Criminal mischief."

He sighed, which is always a weird thing to watch a spirit do, considering they don't actually breathe. "Fine, fine. We'll compromise on criminal mischief."

"I shouldn't have to explain this to you," I said, trying to keep my tone even, "but sometimes, when a witch causes too much mischief, people decide to kill that witch to get them out of the way and stop said mischief."

"Listen, I don't know what she told you, but it's all water under the bridge. The stuff with O'Leary and Malavic, none of it is anything people would want to kill over. That's why I didn't mention it."

"Is that why? Or did you fail to mention it because you didn't want to admit that your actions might have led to your death?"

"Wow," he said. "That angel really did a number on you. Who knew judgment was contagious?"

I decided he might have a point. I *was* being judgmental. I suppose it's a common side effect of feeling like you've been played a fool. "I'll let it go, but will you just be more open with me from now on? We both want the same thing. We want you to move on. Anything you can think of that might provide a clue would be welcome. Sometimes it's the strangest things that prove the best leads."

"Deal. Complete honesty between us from now on."

Eek. I hadn't meant *that*. I had no intention of being completely honest with him. After all, I had a job to do. I needed Dmitri to be honest with me, but in that very moment I was already forming a plan that required keeping him in the dark. Literally.

We walked a few more minutes back toward Ruby's house before I said, "You know, I'm going to be working long hours for the next few days. Maybe you and Grim ought to take the opportunity to do that jaunt in the Deadwoods." I looked from Dmitri to Grim, and both seemed to appreciate the prospect. But I wasn't sure they were sold on it, and I needed them to be. So I sweetened the deal, at least for Grim. "Come on, let's go by the butcher, and I'll pick up some food for you to take with you."

And just like that, I'd bought myself the following afternoon to go interview Greggory O'Leary and Count Sebastian Malavic alone.

Yay?

Some victories sure felt like defeats.

* * *

Greggory O'Leary's home was deep in the heart of Erin Park, which was no surprise; most leprechauns chose to live around their fellows. Safety in numbers and all that.

I didn't know anything about O'Leary, so I decided

against giving him a heads up that I was coming. If he'd had anything to do with Dmitri's death, he was a flight risk.

However, I had my doubts about that theory. Despite what Bloom had said, I didn't think that Dmitri was holding much back in terms of O'Leary. He'd admitted that the two of them had gotten into some dumb trouble. He wasn't hiding that. And I was still mostly of the mind that Dmitri's death was a natural one.

"Hi, Mr. O'Leary," I said when the leprechaun answered his door. "I'm Nora Ashcroft."

"I've heard of ya," he said, eyeing me closely. He was tall for his kind, easily pushing five feet, and his round face was framed by a chestnut colored beard and a short and shaggy mop of hair. A deep, white scar cut from the middle of the cupid's bow of his lips to an inch below his right eye. "You're the Fifth Wind."

"I am."

His tone gave nothing away. "I suppose you'll be wanting to talk to me about Dmitri's death then?"

"That's why I'm here, yes."

"Am I a suspect?"

"Not as far as I'm concerned."

He scoffed. "Then ya might not be too good at your job. If I were you and I knew about me, I'd've come here with handcuffs ready to go."

"I can call Deputy Manchester over here if that's how you want it to go down."

"Nah. I didn't do it anyhow. Well, come on in with ya then."

He stepped to the side and I leaned down to keep from hitting my head on the top of the small door frame.

Thankfully, I didn't have to crouch once I was inside. The ceiling was high enough for guests my size, but the place was still slightly claustrophobic. A thick moss covered the interior walls, only parting around open windows to let the hot afternoon air in.

"Have a seat and I'll put on some tea."

I did, settling myself at a low table in the middle of the living room while he disappeared into the kitchen. I knew from hard-earned experience that hospitality meant nothing particular when it came to this line of work. He could disappear into the kitchen and never come back. Or he could slip something into my tea, like the doppelgängers had, and then lock me in some dreary basement or worse. It was always a possibility.

And because of that, it seemed silly to worry. There were an infinite number of ways someone could harm me, and to imagine all of them in an attempt to stop them was futile and a waste of energy. No matter how much I prepared, bad people found new and surprising ways to get at me. I just had to listen to my Insight and trust that I would find a way to handle things when the worst came to pass.

In the meantime, I might as well accept the hospitality and keep from upsetting the people who could have useful information for me.

O'Leary didn't flee. He returned a few moments later carrying a tray with two wooden cups and a piping hot kettle of tea. He set the cups down, one in front of me and the other at his own seat, placed the kettle between them, then turned to set the tray on a nearby oaken credenza. As he did so, I quickly switched our cups.

What? I might not be able to thwart every attempt, but I wouldn't make it easy for someone to poison me.

He poured us tea, and I made a mental note to wait until he'd had a sip of his to try mine. "How about I save ya some time," he said, leaning back in his chair. "Dmitri didn't have no enemies I knew about, and we haven't gotten into trouble in years."

"Did you know about his heart condition?"

"I wouldn't call it a heart so much as a ticking time bomb."

"When did he tell you about it?"

"As soon as he found out. He came over and said, 'Greg, my life could end tomorrow, and it'd be a shame not to get up to some of the old fun in the meantime.' Well, I told his witchy hide that everyone's life could end tomorrow—that was the way of the world—and that was no reason to up the odds."

"So you talked him out of doing something stupid?"

"Ah, but ya can't talk someone out of doing something stupid. If they had enough sense to listen to reason, they wouldn't be doing stupid things in the first place. And Dmitri was the type of guy who always thought the stupidest things were the smartest of plans."

"And you?"

"I was just stupid enough to go along with him. For the most part."

At least O'Leary wasn't pretending to be above it all. "He said you two hadn't been in trouble in a while."

Finally, he sipped his tea, so I did, too. It was a ruddy color and just strong enough that I thought I could make it through the rest of the afternoon without another cup of coffee.

"Not legal trouble, no," he replied. "We sometimes found ourselves a little bit of it at Sheehan's around closing, though. Especially before Seamus, Lucent, and Slash ended up in Ironhelm." He raised his teacup. "Thanks for that, by the way."

"Don't mention it. I didn't make them steal that gold. They did all the hard work, and I just helped clean it up."

"We need more cleaners in Eastwind, that's for sure. Although Dmitri and I wouldn't've had nearly as much fun if there'd been more of them back then."

"When you two were younger and getting into trouble, what did that look like?"

His gaze wandered the room for a moment, pausing briefly on a packed bookshelf carved from a giant tree stump. "Are ya familiar with leprechaun magic?"

"A little. There was that Guilt Gale that came through last Lunasa Festival."

He chuckled. "Ah, was that what it was? I'd heard rumors, but I wasn't sure. Not summoned one of those myself. I've never found any pleasure in using my magic on others." He paused. "The few times I did, it was just to help us steal a trinket here or there, and it wasn't serious spells."

"And by 'us' you mean you and Dmitri?"

"I do. There's a reason Ezra Ares stopped carrying gold medallions." He grinned, the sun glinting in his hazel eyes. "He also used to use this soft gold wire to secure the crystals for necklaces—but not only is gold a great magical conductor, it's also easy for leprechauns to summon to ourselves when we can get a clear look at it."

"And I take it you did some of that?"

"Sure did. One haul landed Dmitri and me so much

loot, we were able to do a week in Avalon on the profits alone."

"I bet Ezra wasn't too happy about that."

"Ah..." He shrugged and waved me off. "I mean, he wasn't thrilled, but the man admires a good bit of troublemaking, even if it's at his own expense."

"You don't think he's held a grudge since then?"

"Ezra? Not a chance. Especially since we brought him back a few items from Avalon that aren't, strictly speaking, *legal* in this realm."

"He didn't press charges, I take it?" I already knew the answer, though. Sheriff Bloom hadn't mentioned Ezra's name on her list of Dmitri's involvement.

"Of course not. Ezra is a strong supporter of those who skirt the law without outright harming anyone. He wouldn't've wanted to discourage us when we were so young."

"You certainly knew how to keep him quiet."

O'Leary laughed. "Everyone knows how to keep Ezra quiet. It's the same way he keeps everyone else in town quiet about his... *situation*."

He was referring, of course, to the fact that Ezra Ares had stopped aging decades before. I knew a little bit more than most on the topic ever since Donovan's brother had solicited Ezra's help for the same thing, but I wasn't about to divulge any of that right now.

O'Leary went on. "To keep people silent, ya keep them happy. And ya do it in such a way that they don't believe anyone else could do it without too great a personal cost. Ezra has done not-so-legal favors for everyone in power in this town. And he makes his customers feel the same way, like they're getting a deal they can't get anywhere else. We just did the same for him."

"Okay," I said, "enough about Black Market 101. Are you telling me that you and Dmitri just got up to a little leprechaun and witch magic?"

"Not at all. We got up to *a lot* of it. And not always the lighter side."

"Go on."

He shifted in his chair, and his gaze jumped back to the bookshelf for only a split second. "It's called Draíolc. It's the study of dark and ancient magic that leprechauns condemned a while ago. We were by no means practitioners, but we did dabble in it here and there in our stupider years."

"He did, too? Even though he was a witch?"

"Yes. The secrets of this magic are guarded by my kind, but they're available to all those with power."

"What about a Fifth Wind who can't levitate a laundry basket to save her life?"

He chuckled. "Oh, I bet a Fifth Wind could do *quite* well with magic such as this. Necromancy isn't far off from it."

"Sounds lovely," I said. "While you and Dmitri were messing around with the deeply occult, any chance you might have triggered events that led to his death?"

"Most certainly."

I blinked. "O-kay..." I waited for him to continue, but he didn't. "Any specifically that come to mind?"

"All of them might've led to both his death and mine. But none of them did."

"You're sure of that?"

"Fairly. Because we were never really good at

Draíolc. Hardly ever got a spell to work for us. And the ones that did were simple and... mostly harmless."

I took the last sip of my tea without realizing it and got a mouthful of the bitter dregs. Sweet baby jackalope!

O'Leary grinned. "Wakes ya up, doesn't it?"

"Yeah, it does." I set the cup back down gently and tried to regain my focus. But it was too late, and I was pretty sure I had plenty to work from. "I think I'd better get a move on. I have another appointment I shouldn't be late for."

"Of course." We both stood, and he led me out onto the front step.

"If you think of anything that could be useful here, let me know."

He nodded. "And if ya get to the bottom of it, will ya let me know? Dmitri was the best friend I ever had." He sighed heavily. "I can't stand the thought that he might've died of natural causes rather than finding himself neck deep in unicorn swirls of his own making."

"I'll keep you posted."

I turned my back on the leprechaun, wondering if I had any friends who wished the same for me. And if I did, how I could quickly get them out of my life.

Chapter Ten

꽃옆꽃

I couldn't believe I was back at the count's castle. It meant that, since coming to Eastwind, I'd been to a vampire's creepy, isolated home on a peninsula overlooking a deep lake that hid who knew what kind of danger more times than I'd been to a dentist. If gum disease killed me in the end, that would be an irony I deserved.

I'd sent a letter ahead so that the count was expecting me when I knocked. It wasn't great to give someone like him an opportunity to prepare for your arrival on his home turf, but I wasn't a complete idiot; I'd also told Ruby my plans for the day so if I didn't come home, she would know who'd murdered me. Or, more in line with the count's M.O., who had me murdered while keeping his hands nice and clean.

"It's so nice to have visitors," he said, leading me into the gloomy space.

I looked around at the furniture, all red velvet chairs and candles hanging from the ceiling, the wax dripping down the holders. I wanted to call him a walking cliché, but I needed to do my best to stay civil with him until I could learn what I came for about Dmitri.

We entered a sitting room where each portrait on the wall looked like its eyes were following me.

He must have seen me staring, because he said, "You're not imagining it. They're really watching you. I had to order them from Transylvania. A trapped soul in each one." He grinned at my horror. "Kidding, of course. I got them from a tiny market in Dolgoeth. Transylvania is a wasteland with no trace of culture."

He offered me a chair by the fireplace, and though I would have preferred to remain standing, I had to play along.

He helped himself to a small couch with red velvet upholstery, leaning his back against one of the wooden armrests and kicking up his shiny black dress shoes on the other. "What can I help you with today, my dear Nora Ashcroft?"

He knew I was starting at a huge disadvantage. That was the only time he ever acted this friendly. He was savoring it. "I'm curious what you know about Dmitri Flint."

"He's dead." He arched an eyebrow. "Did I get it right?"

"You did. But I mean, what do you know about him from before he died? I understand the two of you had a run-in with the law."

He folded his hands in his lap and tilted his head to the side, pouting out his lips as if I was a thing to be pitied. "Then you understand incorrectly. *He* had a run-in, all right, but before it was with the law, it was with my dragon."

I couldn't disguise my shock. "Your *dragon*? You mean the one that lives behind Rainbow Falls?"

"Yes. And she has a name. It's Maggie. Dmitri and the leprechaun Greggory O'Leary got it in their heads to sneak back there and try to steal some of the town's gold." He observed my mouth hanging open and said, "Oh, come on. You didn't actually think Seamus Shaw was the first leprechaun to get that foolish idea in his head. If he was, there'd be no need to hide the town's treasury behind a raging waterfall and guard it with a dragon."

"Right. It's just that... trying it is so incredibly stupid."

Count Malavic laughed. "Oh yes. I agree with you there. But I'll give Flint and O'Leary credit; they made it past the falls. I still to this day don't know how they managed. But then they injured Maggie, and that was where my amusement ended."

"I can imagine."

"No, you cannot. Thankfully, she got a full swipe across Dmitri's middle. An inch deeper, and she would have gutted him. And he would have deserved it. But as it was, he survived with the proper medical and magical treatment. And Maggie is fine, thanks for asking."

I tried to make sense of it. Dmitri did say he was foolish when he was younger. But this went beyond foolish.

"I pressed charges, obviously," Malavic continued, "beyond what they were already facing for trespassing. No one hurts my dragon and gets away with it."

"And did they?"

"What, get away with it?"

I nodded.

"Mostly. They claimed they only wanted to see a dragon in real life, not rob Eastwind's treasury, and our dearest sheriff must have bought that garbage. They spent a night in jail, were assigned community service, and then released."

"I bet that made you angry," I said.

"If you're wondering whether it made me angry enough to murder Dmitri, the answer is no. Besides, I have an alibi for that night. I was at Sheehan's during the time in which he died. It couldn't have been me."

"You could have hired someone."

He chuckled and clasped his hands behind his head. "So true. Darkness knows I can afford it. But I could have done it a number of times in the years since he pulled his stunt with O'Leary. Why wait until now? It doesn't make any sense."

"It doesn't, which is precisely why you would have waited this long."

The count rolled his eyes. "I may have endless time to spare, but even I'm not *that* patient for a little revenge. No, I called it even once they were assigned community service."

"That doesn't sound like you."

"That's because you don't know what that community service *was*." His top lip twitched in suppressed pleasure. "Both fools were required to clean up my dragon's droppings... while I supervised. Let's just say a few things I fed her that week might not have agreed with her stomach."

"Say no more. Please."

The count shrugged a single shoulder but changed the subject. "It wouldn't surprise me if O'Leary had something to do with Flint's death. Assuming, of course, that foul play was involved at all."

"I already spoke with O'Leary. He didn't mention anything that sounded promising."

"I bet he also failed to mention the dragon situation." He knew he had me there, and his dry chuckle was like nails on a chalkboard. "He did, didn't he? But that seemed incredibly relevant to your case only a moment ago. And yet, he didn't think to mention it. I bet Dmitri, assuming you've met with him, also failed to mention it. What *else* is the spirit hiding from you?"

"Nuh-uh," I said. "You've pulled this one on me before, and you're not doing it again."

He raised one of his dagger-like brows. "Pulled what on you before?"

"You know what. Insinuating things about someone, implying that there's a lot more to the story they're hiding from me." To be fair, Bloom had done the same, but she had been more forthcoming about her implications. And I didn't loathe her.

"It's usually the case, though. Have I been wrong?"

"Yes," I said, feeling victorious. "A few months ago, you tried to imply that Donovan might have said something to Eva that made her jump through the portal, knowing Tanner would follow her through."

His stony expression gave nothing away. "And?"

"It wasn't true. I asked him what was said, and... he never wanted that to happen."

"I'm sure he told you that." The count stood, and I

was left with the tough choice of following his lead or staring up at him.

I stood.

"Since we're on the topic of your little love triangle," he said, "and I've made it plain even to someone of your low-grade intelligence that I had no interest in murdering Dmitri Flint, there's something I think you ought to see."

"I can't imagine you have anything that would interest me, Malavic. No offense." Yes offense.

"None taken." I could tell he took some. "Right this way, Ms. Ashcroft."

As he made swiftly for a dim hallway, I paused, trying to decide what to do. Whatever he was about to show me was likely bad news. But my curiosity was killing me. And how bad could it be?

Stupid question.

I followed him out of the room and through the dark and narrow stone corridor. When he turned and descended a set of stairs, I wondered if I was actually crazy for following the town's only vampire into what was surely a dungeon.

Yes, Ruby knew where I was, but that would only help to ensure retribution if anything happened to me, it wouldn't keep anything from happening to me in the first place.

Oh well, gotta die sometime.

I took my time on the stairs that were smooth from age and use.

The count was waiting for me at the bottom, wearing a smugger than usual expression. "All I ask," he said, "is that you don't act irrationally when you see what I'm about to show you."

I raised my chin, giving him my iciest stare. "I promise nothing."

He sighed. "That's about what I expected."

The room wouldn't have looked out of place carrying an array of torture devices, but as it was, it seemed to be more of a study, with stone shelves housing books and no-doubt expensive bottles of red wine. There were two high-backed chairs, also with velvet upholstery, but this time black instead of red. The space was lit only by a few bobbing and enchanted orbs in each corner that cast a soft glow and created faint, dancing shadows across the floor and walls.

A violet drape hovered in midair only a few feet to the left of one of the chairs. Malavic positioning himself to the side of the cloth and waited until he had my full attention.

Once he did, he placed a hand on the top of the drape. "And this is what I thought you ought to see."

He yanked away the covering, and the second the light hit my eyes, I felt my heart fall into my feet.

No way. It couldn't be.

Chapter Eleven

The space where the violet cloth had just hung, suspended in midair, was now a bright patch of sunlight. I let my eyes adjust and felt like punching Sebastian Malavic right in the jaw when I saw the familiar landscape stretching out beyond the mouth of the portal between worlds.

"If that leads to where I think it leads," I ground out between clenched teeth.

He threw his arms into the air. "Of course it does! Why else would I show you?"

His face was looking more punchable by the second, but I planted my feet on the cold stone floor beneath me to keep from doing anything dangerous to my continued mortal existence. "How long has it been open?" I demanded. "It could completely topple the natural balance between the realms and—"

"Three hundred and twenty-five years."

I gaped at him. "Oh."

"I opened it very slowly and carefully over a period of

NOVA NELSON

a decade," he said. "And nobody noticed the imbalance with a war going on."

"Or maybe your portal caused an imbalance that contributed to the war."

He dismissed it with a wave of his hand. "Semantics, really."

"Not even a little bit."

But it was obvious that nothing I could say would add a drop of guilt to his veins.

He said, "Nature adjusted, anyhow, and equilibrium has yet been achieved with no resulting catastrophe. At least none that can conclusively be attributed to this."

I continued staring through the portal. Judging by the shadows on the other side, it was midday there. I'd noticed this anomaly in the last portal I found myself staring through, that the times of day didn't quite match. It had been night on both sides when I'd first died and come to Eastwind, but that seemed to be more of a coincidence than the rule with inter-realm travel. "And it leads back to Texas?"

"No, no. It leads to Louisiana."

I couldn't believe it. "*My* Louisiana?"

He scoffed. "I hardly think you can claim it as yours."

"But you mean the Louisiana in my old world, right? This isn't another Wisconsin situation?"

"In terms you'll understand, yes, this portal leads back to the world in which you were born. And the world in which Tanner and Eva have been living quite safely since they left Eastwind."

"You... How do you... How long have you..." I couldn't formulate a dozen questions at once, and they all seemed equally important. So naturally, the most irrelevant one popped out. "Have you been going between realms? Is *that* how you know pop-culture references from my old world?"

He clasped his hands in front of him and tilted his head to the side. "Well done, ten points to Gryffindor."

I'd never have believed a perfectly executed Harry Potter reference could leave me so furious. But there it was.

I returned my attention to the circular window leading to Louisiana.

Tanner was out there somewhere. I could step through and find him. I could make a run for it and not look back!

Huh, that was probably the irrational behavior the count had requested I refrain from indulging. Or maybe he'd meant something more along the lines of what I did next.

I stepped forward, closing the distance between the portal and myself, and smacked Sebastian Malavic across the face so hard, I busted his lip on one of his fangs.

His shock only lasted for a millisecond before it warped into pleasure, which only made me want to slap him again, and harder. But instead, I got in his face, pointing a finger an inch from his nose, and hissed, "You've been waiting, haven't you? You just want to make me miserable, so you waited until I was settled into my new life with Donovan, until I'd finally started to move on from Tanner, before you dumped this on me. Admit it, you were just waiting for the worst possible time." My hands were shaking, and I tried to will them to stop so he didn't get the satisfaction of knowing just how much he'd gotten to me.

He held up his hands in a sign of surrender. "I admit it. And why wouldn't I?" He licked the dark blood from his lips. Was that his blood or the blood of a recent snack? "I haven't had a beautiful woman slap me like that in centuries. Wouldn't change a thing, to be honest."

Had it also been centuries since a woman had kneed him right in his balls? Because I would have been happy to accommodate him. But that might be pushing things too far. It ran the risk of making him truly angry at me, which was dangerous. Or he might enjoy it far more than the slap, which was worse.

So instead, I decided to deprive him of the one thing he craved so badly. I couldn't change what had already happened, but I could keep from giving him any more satisfaction from my response. I cast one last look at the glowing gateway, feeling a weight in my chest pull me toward it, toward Tanner, wherever he was, and then I turned on my heel and marched out of the count's castle without saying another word.

I made it all the way off the narrow peninsula and to the edge of town before I collapsed on a stone bench and put my head in my hands. It'd been so long since I'd cried, having grown sick of it quickly after Tanner left and swearing it off, I was worried that it wouldn't come, that I wouldn't be able to relieve the pressure building in my chest and I would simply explode. But nope, there were the tears.

I like to get all my crying done at once. It's an efficient way to handle emotions. But it means ugly crying and a whopping dose of self-pity condensed into a short amount of time. Thankfully, I'd mastered this technique; my life had never accommodated general weepiness.

And so the self-pity tumbled down on me in an avalanche.

What was I supposed to do? I had started this new life with Donovan. I had already gone through the worst of the pain of losing Tanner, and now would I have to relive it all over again? I didn't want to make this choice! I didn't want this choice to exist!

But then again, it could mean finding Tanner. Didn't I want that? The five of us in our circle couldn't all be in the same realm again, that was clear. The power we possessed was too strong and would upset the balance like it had before, causing all kinds of terror.

But I could go through. I could leave Landon here with Grace, and I could go.

And so could Donovan. He could come with me, and he could find Eva and bring her back.

If she wanted to come back.

Maybe he would stay there, and Tanner could come with me back to Eastwind. Did I even want to return to Eastwind? Did I want to be back in Texas?

It was all too confusing, and I hated it. But if I wasn't careful, my confusion would make me lose focus and I'd end my crying prematurely, before it was all out.

Get it together, Ashcroft! Are you here to cry your eyes out or not?!

I was. So I steeled my mind and refocused on the pity party. There were streamers, a cake, a piñata—the works.

Finally, when I couldn't squeeze out any more tears, I wiped my nose on my sleeve, dried my eyes, and took a few deep breaths.

I didn't have to make a decision right now. Malavic

said the gateway had been open for over three hundred years. It would stay open for a while longer.

My sense began to return. Sweet baby jackalope, did this new discovery complicate everything. However, after the release, my desire to drive a stake through Malavic's heart was somewhat lessened.

Somewhat.

Just as I stood from my crying spot, still red-eyed, though there wasn't much to be done about that, an owl came out of the blue. Literally. It swooped down from the sky and perched on the branch of a nearby tree, hooting at me until I took the hint.

Still sniffling, I grabbed the piece of parchment from its talons, and unfolded the letter. I recognized Stu Manchester's scribbled writing. It simply said, *Miss Ashcroft. Medical examiner's done. Something you might want to see. Come quick.*

Chapter Twelve

I caught a reflection of myself in the glass doors of the Sheriff's Department and saw that my eyes were still unmistakably bloodshot.

Oh well. If Stu asked, I'd just tell him I'd been doing drugs. He wouldn't want to know more for fear of having to arrest his only help out in the field.

Jingo nodded for me to pass and seemed somewhat in lighter spirits when he saw that Grim wasn't with me.

I knocked on Stu's door, and he answered right away as if he'd been waiting just on the other side for the sound. "This way, Ms. Ashcroft. The MedEx just took her coffee break, so we have a little time to ourselves before she comes back to prep for the MagEx."

I'll be honest, I wasn't a fan of the examination room. It was located in the underground section of the station, near where they kept the evidence lockers. The room had an observation window overlooking it from the hallway, but we just walked right in and up to the iron table on which the covered body lie. Dmitri's body.

A stark light hovered overhead, too blinding to look anywhere near it, but I was sure it would provide plenty of illumination to see every nook and cranny of whatever person was unfortunate enough to be on display below it.

Stu stepped to one side, and I took the other. Slowly, he pulled the sheet back, and I braced myself for the worst. I knew just enough about medical examiners back home to know there was some cutting and sawing involved with the process, and refined sewing skills never seemed to be a job requirement. So I was pleasantly surprised when I saw that Dmitri hadn't gone through any of that treatment. Of course not. He might have only seen the medical examiner so far and not the magical examiner, but that didn't mean the medical examiner didn't have anything magical with which to gaze into the patient.

Was "patient" the word for it at this point? Seemed incongruent with rigor mortis.

There was something unsettling about how familiar his face was to me. It was like looking at an old friend, except this was the first time I'd ever gazed at his real face. I'd probably passed him in town, maybe been at Sheehan's with him at the same time, but his had just been an anonymous face in the crowd to me. Just backdrop to whatever drama was swirling in my life at the time.

But he was like a friend now—no, he *was* a friend. Unfortunately, that hadn't developed while he was still alive. And the man I was looking down at, did I even know him?

Stu cleared his throat. "The MedEx said it looked pretty clear that his heart giving out was the cause of death. I won't go into the grisly details, but suffice it to say, the signs were all there."

"He had a heart condition that he knew about, so that adds up."

Stu nodded. "There were a few slashes along the torso, but they were all scarred up, so they couldn't have been the cause." He lowered the sheet as far as it could go without compromising Dmitri's modesty, and I took in the scratches.

"Malavic's dragon got him there."

"That's what Bloom suggested when I ran them by her."

"What's that?" I asked, pointing at an intricate symbol in black ink over his failed heart.

"That's what I wanted to ask you, actually. I was wondering if you could ask him if it had any significance."

My Insight kicked me in the seat of my pants, and in an attempt to assuage it, I stared at the marking harder. "I recognize it, but I can't think of where from."

"Is he here right now? Can you ask him?"

"Huh?" I looked up from the body. "Oh, no. He's in the Deadwoods with Grim for the day." I gazed back down at the symbol, obsidian against the tan of his chest. It was all curves and loops, like a Celtic knot with no obvious beginning or end. Where had I seen it before? Was I just imagining the connection? Or was it a knot I'd perhaps seen in a past life, whether in Texas or Ireland?

"It could just be a design he liked," I suggested.

Stu grunted. "People don't just mark themselves with pretty designs."

"In my old world they did."

"Sounds foolish and risky. Body markings always carry a significance. Whether this is some sort of gang or group he belongs to or... I don't know. I just have a feeling it's important."

I nodded. "I can certainly ask him about it when I see him again." I ran my hand over it and felt a jolt run through my arm. Strange. "It's right over his heart."

"The heart that gave out, yes."

"Maybe it's some kind of protection."

"I think you'd better just ask him."

"If it carries any kind of, I don't know, magical significance, wouldn't the magical examiner pick up on that?"

"He would. But Brightburn's been in Avalon all week and won't see the body for another couple of days. And if it's just to mark affiliation, he might not pick up anything. Nevertheless, I believe it's important to the homicide investigation."

Homicide investigation? I jerked back to get a better look at him. "I thought you said he died of natural causes. Of his heart stopping."

"I said his heart stopping was the cause of death, but that doesn't mean it's natural."

I wasn't convinced. While I was always suspicious that there was something sinister behind every strange occurrence in Eastwind—experience had taught me that —there was still no actual evidence supporting the theory of foul play. And there was quite a bit of circumstantial evidence supporting the story that Dmitri had a heart condition and his number had finally been called.

I felt suddenly antsy. I'd seen all I'd needed to, and I

didn't want to spend a second more in the presence of the corpse.

And it just went to show how much Stu Manchester trusted me that he allowed me to be in the same room with a deceased after I'd taken over the body of Donovan's uncle only a few months before. To be fair, I'd had a solid reason for that. But it's quite a thing to know that you can no longer truthfully claim, "I've never worn a dead guy around town." People don't generally overlook that sort of behavior, either. Especially not law enforcement. But I got a pass because I'd made myself useful enough. Thank Gaia for that.

"Can we wrap this up?" I said, before begrudgingly adding, "No pun intended."

Stu brought the sheet back up to cover Dmitri's face and escorted me out of the room. Once we were back upstairs, he stopped me before I could sprint home, and said, "There's something else."

"Yes?"

"I, um... You know I'm not great with emotions, Ms. Ashcroft. But I consider you a friend, and as your friend, I couldn't help but notice your eyes were awfully red when you came into the station."

I swallowed down the traitorous lump in my throat and let him continue.

"Is everything all right?"

"More than all right."

"It looks like you've been crying."

Drugs, I thought. *Tell him about the drugs.*

But Stu *was* my friend. I didn't want to worry him further by convincing him that he needed to stage some sort of intervention. Besides, I wasn't sure what the drug scene was like in this realm. I wasn't even sure they had them, and if they did, what those drugs did.

"You're right. I was crying."

He cringed. "Is it anything I can help with?"

"Only if you feel like walking over to Widow Lake and driving a stake through Count Malavic's heart."

"Ah." He tilted his head back and didn't ask any more questions. "Well, you take care of yourself."

Chapter Thirteen

Grim jumped up from his favorite spot on the front porch as I approached. It was nearly dark, so at first, I couldn't make out if it was him or if some creature from the Murderswamp had gotten lost and wandered into town.

"Ruby won't let me inside!" I could tell from the tone of his thoughts that he'd been agonizing over this fact for hours.

"That's because you look like you spent the day rolling in mud."

As he wagged his tail, a clump of the muck flew off and stuck to the armrest of the porch swing. *"I did. The Deadwoods have the best mud. Years of death and decay mixed in. Everyone knows that."*

I paused a safe distance from him and assessed the damage.

His tail drooped and he lowered his head. *"Will you help me?"*

"Fine."

I opened the front door and saw Ruby and Dmitri

sitting at the parlor table, chatting pleasantly with one another.

"You're back," Ruby said. "I was starting to wonder if the count had finally managed to properly seduce you."

Dmitri chuckled.

But I just glared. "Seduce? Not a chance. But we'll get back to him. Can Grim come into the bathroom to get cleaned off?"

It took a little convincing and a promise on my part that I would personally scrub up all the muddy paw prints after the fact, but Ruby finally agreed. I'd like to take full credit for the persuasive victory, but I'm positive Dmitri's friendly presence worked in Grim's favor, too.

Once the clean up was complete, Grim joined Clifford by the cool, blue fire, and Monster quickly curled herself up in his warm fur. A hot cup of tea was already waiting for me once I'd disposed of the muddy rag I'd used to scrub the paw prints. It was times like these when I most regretted not possessing the kind of magic that made this sort of menial task disappear with the flick of a wand.

"So," Dmitri said, "you saw the count today."

"Oh, right." I paused. How much did he suspect about the timing? Only one way to find out: "I just had some time free, and I figured why wait?"

"You mean you had me out of the way, so you took the opportunity to go interview people about me."

I opened my mouth to respond, but he held up a transparent hand and said, "Don't worry. Ruby already made a strong case for why that was the right decision."

"Ah." I turned to her. "Thanks."

She nodded gently.

"So?" Dmitri prompted. "Learn anything of interest?"

Fangs and claws, had I! But the portal wasn't relevant to my investigation, and telling them probably wasn't a great idea...

And yet, there I was, already halfway through the story by the time my good sense caught up.

"He wasn't even shy about the fact that he'd waited six months just to cause me more psychological anguish!"

Ruby said, "Of course he wasn't shy about that. He's not shy or ashamed about anything. It's a gift of his."

"Gift for him, curse for the rest of us." I fell silent for a moment, feeling myself run out of steam for the day. "It's not fair. If he'd just shown it to me on November first, there'd be no decision to make! I would have sprinted through it faster than you can say 'reckless.' But no. He waits just long enough until I'm starting to put my life back together. Ugh! I bet he saw me and Donovan together at the scufflepuck tournament, noticed how happy we were, and decided now was the time to pull this nonsense, now that we have a solid foundation."

"You have a solid foundation with Donovan?" Dmitri asked. "That's news to me."

"Ha-ha," I said dryly. "I mean, as solid of a foundation as anyone can have with Donovan."

Ruby added, "Was this the same scufflepuck tournament where Donovan was trying to pick a fight with a genie? Where *the count* had to step in and finally put a stop to it? Was *that* the one where you two were so happy together?"

I narrowed my eyes at her but said nothing, only sipped my tea.

But they weren't going to let me off that easy. Dmitri said, "Out of curiosity, when was the last time you spoke with him?"

I felt my face flush as I tried to remember. Today was Wednesday, and we'd last spoken on Sunday, when we'd gone for a casual bite at Franco's on his night off. I'd filled him in on the fact that, yes, the dead guy had shown up at my bedroom window, and no, he hadn't laid a hand on me. It'd been an oddly pleasant night together with very little friction. And perhaps because of that, very little passion. When I'd yawned over my fettuccini alfredo, he'd laughed good-naturedly and walked me home. It struck me as particularly Tanner-like behavior—caring, not needy—and the fact that he'd simply kissed me, bid me goodnight, and left without asking to come upstairs left me boggled.

Though, to be fair, the last time I'd invited Donovan upstairs had been a disaster. Monster, it seemed, felt the need to defend her witch's honor by making sure Tanner's best friend and I didn't have a fun moment alone in his absence, if she had anything to do with it. Donovan had been lucky to escape with all his limbs that night. So maybe that explained it.

Anyway, that made it three days since we'd last spoken. Was three days too long for a happy couple to go without speaking?

But instead of asking that and possibly giving Dmitri the satisfaction of being right, I said, "What are you, my relationship counselor?"

He shrugged. "I guess so, if we're going off of the fact that you just spent the last five minutes painting your romantic dilemma in vivid detail for us."

Ruby lifted her teacup to her lips to try to hide her giggle.

"Oh, you're so funny," I said, knowing he had a strong point.

Suddenly, a strange scratching noise caught my attention, and I turned toward the front door where it was coming from.

"I tried to talk her out of it," Grim said. *"But she won't listen to reason!"*

It was Monster. The munchkin cat was clawing at the front door like she'd resigned herself to digging right through it if no one opened it for her. And by the looks of it, she'd succeed.

"What's she doing?" Dmitri asked.

The realization hit me like a wand to the sternum. "Monster is Tanner's familiar. She was left behind. They've been separated for months."

Dmitri nodded and stared down at the table. "She wants to go to him." His shoulders drooped. "My Maverick is at the sanctuary already. Bryant took her in yesterday."

My heart sank even further. I'd actually forgotten all about that specific tragedy.

Dmitri, aside from being dead, was a witch. Which meant he'd had a familiar. And when he'd died, she'd been left behind.

I scrambled for something to say to make him (and myself) feel better. "Zoe Clementine takes amazing care of the animals. I'm sure Maverick is as comfortable as she can be."

He shook his head, wispy tracers resulting from the

movement. "That doesn't sound like Mav. She's a terror. I mostly feel sorry for Zoe."

Oh. "I can go check on her tomorrow, if you'd like."

He lifted his chin. "No need. I've already dropped in a few times. She's doing okay. She knew this day was coming, just like I did. She'd promised me she'd give hell to whoever got her next, and that's all I can hope for."

Sheesh, poor Zoe.

Ruby said, "Someone really ought to keep that cat from tunneling out." She looked squarely at me.

"Pssh! No way. Have you seen the claws on her? I have a feeling she's been waiting her whole life for an opportunity to kill a large animal, and I'm not about to sacrifice myself for that cause." I turned to Grim. *"You owe me for that bath. Handle your friend."*

To my surprise, he didn't argue, but instead stomped across the room and snatched her up in his jaws by her scruff. She hissed and tried to take a swipe at him, but her little munchkin cat legs couldn't reach at that angle, and she gave up before long. Her body dangled limply from his jaw, exposing her little pink potbelly.

"I think it's time for bed," Grim said before marching them both upstairs.

Once they were out of sight, Dmitri said, "Have you told Donovan yet?"

Ruby arched an eyebrow like this soap opera was just getting good.

"No. I haven't had a chance. But I don't think I'm going to tell him about it."

"You're not?" he said.

"Why would I? It'll just make him insecure."

"Or," he said, "maybe he'd want to know that he could go find his best friend and previous girlfriend."

Even worse.

"I doubt that would be his first thought," I replied. "He's not a hero like Tanner, and I don't say that to disparage him. Tanner's heroics started this whole mess."

"Heroics usually do," Ruby said before sipping her tea.

"Either way," he added, "is it really up to you to keep that from him? Shouldn't you tell him the truth and let him do with it what he will? He has to make the best choices for himself."

I knew he was right. But I also knew telling Donovan that there was a doorway that could lead me back to Tanner wouldn't work out well for anyone. I already wished I could forget it.

Especially because I had no plans of going through. My portal hopping had already caused enough trouble in Eastwind. I didn't need to keep messing with the balance.

And it didn't help that the last time I'd found myself in this sort of situation was when I'd come clean with Tanner about what had gone on with me and Donovan. He'd broken up with me not long after that. Sure, we'd gotten back together, so one might say things turned out in the end... depending on where you marked the end. If you pushed that marker a little farther out, past the point where Tanner jumped through after Eva, then things *didn't* turn out so great between us.

"You're right," I finally said. "But I'm calling it right now: it's going to ruin everything. So now it's just a matter of deciding when I'm ready to devastate my relationship with Donovan in the name of truth." I sighed and shook my head. "Fangs and claws, I hate honesty."

"If it's any comfort," Ruby said, "most people do. Lying is usually a much pleasanter experience on the whole."

The only sound that could be heard now were Clifford's soft snores.

It was only then that I remembered I had other important business to attend to. Business that wasn't all about me.

I turned to face Dmitri. "I saw your body today."

If that upset him, his expression didn't show it. "I hope they respected my modesty. But if they didn't, you're welcome."

I rolled my eyes. "Don't be a creep."

"You're the one staring at my dead body."

"Okay, fair enough." I ran over the pertinent facts in my head, but my brain was running slow. Finally, I said, "I wanted to ask you about that tattoo on your chest."

"Ah yes." His translucent form was growing more difficult to see, even while the parlor stayed dim. He would need to disappear for a while soon to recharge his energy. "That was one of those less intelligent decisions from my youth."

"Did O'Leary have anything to do with it?"

"No. He didn't know about it, as far as I'm aware. We were close, but we didn't undress in front of each other."

"What about swimming? Maybe you took your shirt off and he was there?"

But he pouted his lips, then said, "No. The leisure activities we did with other friends. Any time we got together, we were up to fully clothed mischief. And once

I reformed my ways, we usually had a pint and relived the glory days."

"So, what does it mean?"

He shrugged, and the movement caused his shoulders to dissipate completely for a moment. "Oh, just a little token of love from my younger years." He smiled, but it didn't quite reach his eyes. "Like I said, not one of my more intelligent decisions."

"Love for who?"

"My childhood sweetheart. I was so sure that we were meant to be together. But if that was the case, it would have happened before I'd died, wouldn't it?" He chuckled.

"I suppose there's a logic to that." I paused. "Is this why you give me so much dating advice? You're trying to help me because it didn't work out for you?"

"There's a good chance that's the case. But I stopped pining for her years ago. I do still think of her fondly from time to time, as all adults do of their first love, but any thoughts of a reunion are long lost."

Parts of him began to disappear in patches and reappear slowly.

Was this all there was to it? What about the jolt I'd felt when I'd run my hand over it? "I just thought I recognized the symbol."

"It's possible you did. It's not an uncommon symbol for commemorating that sort of life event."

"What, love?"

"No. Loss of love."

Before I could ask any more questions, he said, "We can speak more in the morning. I don't have much left in me tonight."

Ruby and I bid him goodnight, and I waited until I was sure no more whisps of him might be lingering. Then I turned to her and said, "I'm sure the tattoo is important."

"How do you know?"

"My Insight started kicking me in the rear end the moment I laid eyes on it."

Ruby nodded. "Right answer."

"But I can't seem to get at what it's trying to tell me. The connection is there, just out of reach." I paused. "You mentioned that you sometimes meditate to access your Insight more directly."

"Yes, that's one of the weapons in my Fifth Wind arsenal. Are you interested in learning?"

"If it helps me figure this out."

Ruby set down her mug and looked at me squarely. "Are you telling me that you don't trust Dmitri and that you think there's something more going on here?"

"Don't get me wrong, I like him. But even good people can do stupid things. So, no, I don't trust him to tell me everything."

"Well, thank the goddess for that! I haven't just been talking to the wall for the last year and a half." She stood from her chair. "Come. You'll need to get more comfortable if you're to have any chance of learning this." She led me over to her reading chair and gestured for me to sit.

I gaped at her. I hadn't had the courage to sit in that chair even once since coming to stay with her. It seemed so obvious that it was for her and her alone that I'd considered it Ruby's Chair from day one.

She motioned for me to sit again, this time more

adamantly. "Come now, it's not cursed." Then, as a mere footnote, "...Anymore."

I did as she said and found it more comfortable than I would have guessed. The permanent groove from her backside was impossible to miss, and too large for mine to fill, but it made the experience nice and ergonomic, I suppose.

She placed her soft blanket over my legs, and I immediately understood the appeal of it. For a ridiculous moment, I could see myself in this exact spot thirty years from now. Ruby might be gone by then, and I'd have taken over her post. Maybe I would have a young and reckless Fifth Wind living with me to train as well. And no man in my life—not Tanner or Donovan or anyone.

The image was surprisingly pleasant.

"Now listen up," Ruby said. "This is not an easy skill, but it *is* an important one, and for someone of your impatience, I imagine it won't come naturally."

I took the jabs with as much grace as I could (it helped being so cozy) and then the real training began.

Chapter Fourteen

The following morning was spent managing Medium Rare's unusually vibrant Thursday breakfast crowd and searching for spare moments to practice the meditation techniques Ruby had done her best to teach me the night before.

She'd been right, though, I was probably a lost cause. Relaxation was just never my thing, and apparently that was a big part of opening one's mind. Go figure.

Needless to say, I did *not* tap into my Insight and unlock the mystery of Dmitri's tattoo. But the more I considered the thing in the light of day, the more I began to believe that it was either a symbol I'd seen randomly somewhere else before or it looked so much like a basic Celtic knot that my mind was playing tricks on me.

It also didn't help my concentration that, in every spare moment I had between taking and delivering orders, Grim and Dmitri talked my ear off about their trip to the Deadwoods the day before.

Mostly, the two of them got me when I went behind

the counter to make a fresh pot of coffee.

"I saw it, Nora!" Dmitri proclaimed on one such errand. "I can't even believe it, but I saw a hidebehind!"

Trying not to move my lips too much, I said, "I thought the whole deal was that you never saw them because they always *hide behind* something when you look."

"Well, sure, but I guess they can't sense spirits."

That wasn't entirely impossible, but I was still skeptical. This had tall tale written all over it. "And what'd it look like?"

He brought his ghostly hand to his chin to recall. "Long, slender, furry..."

"You sure it wasn't an otter?"

His lips pressed into a thin line and he squinted at me. "You don't believe me. But I swear it on my life."

"I hope you'll excuse me if I don't take that to mean much."

"Oh. Right." He shook his head to clear it. "All these figures of speech stop making sense once you're dead. But I will say this: I've never felt so alive."

I chuckled. "Probably helps that you weren't in any real danger out there."

He shrugged in noncommittal agreement just as Grim spoke up from his designated spot beneath the countertop. *"Not even a little bit true. He almost got attacked by a soul swallow like three times and didn't even know it."*

"What's a soul swallow?"

Grim raised his heavy head, his ears perking up in excitement. *"Exactly what it sounds like! A creature that swallows souls."*

I rinsed out the empty coffee pot and stuck it back in the cradle. *"That sounds disastrous."*

"It would have been if he hadn't been with me. I saved him."

I flicked on one of the coffeemakers and dumped the old grinds from the second. *"Oh yeah? And how'd you manage that?"*

"Knowledge, Nora. I happened to know the one thing that repels soul swallows."

"And that is?"

"Hellhound urine."

"Grim, that repels everything.*"*

The stories continued like that, each slightly less credible than the last, and while I did find them entertaining, they kept me from getting a moment of peace until well into the afternoon.

Jane came in for her shift just as I was wrapping up my accounting from the day's sales so far. She was half an hour early as she knocked lightly on the manager's office door and then let herself in.

The sound startled me out of my mental fog of numbers. "Oh hey, coming for a bite?"

"Yep. You want me to put in an order for you with Anton while I'm at it?"

Typically, my answer would be "Hellhound, yes," and "my usual," which was a Sunrise Burger with the egg on top cooked over easy, some melted queso for sliced cheese, and a side of truffle fries. Were it not for the fact that I was always active on my feet for 8-10 hours before each of these indulgent meals, there wouldn't have been a chance I would still fit into any of the clothes I'd bought when I first came to town.

"Not today," I said. "Got plans."

"Date night?"

"Yep." I finished filling in the total at the bottom of the sheet, and then stood and grabbed my bag from the back of the chair. "Mind if I take off early?"

"Not if you don't mind me eating my food in peace and letting the kids handle the front of house for a while."

"Deal."

"Where's he taking you? Somewhere fancy?"

I grimaced. I already knew what she'd say, but I told her anyway. "Franco's Pizza."

She groaned and leaned a shoulder against the door frame, crossing her arms over her chest. "He's taking you to his work?"

"He said he doesn't mind being there."

"Right, but it's not exactly romantic to take your girlfriend to your place of employment. Can't he at least take you to Stews and Brews?"

"Nooo," I said, "because that's where Tanner and I used to go."

She threw her arms into the air in exasperation. "You two used to go everywhere!" She lowered her voice and frowned at me. "Nora, I'm not going to tell you how to mourn, but it's in your best interest to create new memories over the old. After Bruce died... well, I had a lot of mixed feelings, as you know. And my impulse was the same as yours. But if I'd followed through with it, I wouldn't have been able to come back here to work, and Ansel and I would also only be able to go out to eat at Franco's Pizza."

"They have great lasagna," I protested lamely.

"Right. But hell is eating your favorite food over and

over again until it makes you want to scream."

I didn't know much about hell, so I didn't argue.

Jane stepped forward and placed a gentle hand on my arm. "Tanner's gone, Nora. No one misses him quite like you do, but we all still miss him. I've known him a long time, and I love him. But people leave us. And even though you might be able to talk to some of them for a little while after that, everyone eventually goes and doesn't come back. Losing people is just part of life."

"You don't understand," I said.

"I do. You're saving space for him. People do it all the time. Maybe someone doesn't sit in the chair at the dinner table where their loved one always used to sit, or maybe a husband sleeps on the same side of the bed as always, even though he now has plenty of room in the middle. But as long as you hold space like that, you're not making room for other things."

I understood what she was saying all too well. After my parents were murdered, I'd returned to my house only once to collect my things. I'd wanted to take my mother's favorite pair of diamond earrings with me—not because of the value, but because of the significance—but I couldn't bring myself to remove them from the small jewelry bowl she kept next to her bathroom sink. What if she came home and couldn't find them? They needed to stay exactly where they were, everything did, so my parents could pick up right where they left off. So my life could pick up right where it left off.

"I hear what you're saying," I told her, "and I don't disagree. But like I said, you don't understand. Tanner's not gone forever." I hesitated before saying the rest. But if I could tell a stranger's ghost about it, I could muster the courage to tell my best friend. "There's another portal to my old world. Count Malavic just showed me yesterday."

Her hand dropped from my arm and her mouth fell open. "Mother Moon," she breathed. "That changes everything, doesn't it?"

"Yep."

She scrunched her nose then asked, "What are you going to do?"

I wanted to stick to my guns, to say I was definitely staying in Eastwind, that this new development didn't change anything.

But instead, I told the truth. "I don't know."

She nodded slowly. "Yeah, I wouldn't know what to do either. You have an impossible choice to make, I think."

I sighed and sat back down, and she grabbed another chair from the wall and pulled it over to sit across from me.

"What do you think I should do?"

She held up her hands. "Noooo, no, no. I'm not telling you what I think, because then if you do it and it blows up in your face, you'll be able to blame me." Then she added, "But I will say that if you decide to go find Tanner and Eva, I'll come along."

My eyes shot open. I had *not* been expecting that. Although, maybe I should have been. "Come along? Like, through the portal?"

"Yeah. I'm not scared of portals. And your world sounds pretty tame. Remember, I've been to Wisconsin and lived to tell the tale. I think I can handle... what were those things you mentioned once that put holes in people?"

"Guns?"

"Right. I think I can handle guns. Sound safer than the wands these lunatic witches wave around."

Jane's offer was almost enough to convince me that we should close Medium Rare for the night and venture into Louisiana right that second. She was literally the most dangerous bitch (her word, not mine) that I knew. Tracking down our lost friends seemed all but done if I had Jane with me.

But it still presented the problem of having Tanner back in my life.

"I'll let you know if I decide to go," I said, "but don't hold your breath. I think I'd be better off just figuring out how to close the thing and moving on with my life."

She patted my knee and got to her feet. "My offer stands."

I got up from my seat, too. "What about Ansel?"

She arched an eyebrow at me. "What about him?"

"Will he be okay with you going?"

"We'd find out as soon as I came back, I'm sure. Most likely, he'll be glad for a little alone time with his bestie Darius."

I followed her out into the hall, and before she headed to the kitchen and I left out the back, she said, "I don't think there's a right answer to your dilemma. But maybe that means there's not a wrong answer either."

While I appreciated the sentiment behind the idea, I said, "If there *is* a wrong answer, you can count on me to pick it."

She chuckled. "No one's ever said you weren't dependable."

Chapter Fifteen

Donovan and I had snagged a table along the wall farthest from the entrance to Franco's, halfway between the bar and the front windows, and we held hands across the table while he refilled my glass of red wine from the bottle.

How could the moment be so divine and so full of dread all at once?

"And Trinity didn't mind you kicking him out?" I asked in response to the story he'd just told.

He grinned. "Not at all. One flick of the wand and he was out the door. Trinity slipped me a silver for it. Don't let the fairy fool you, she seems sweet, but there's a reason she was made manager after Jane left. She's just as fierce as a werewolf bitch."

"No way," I said. "There's no way she's as terrifying as Jane, no matter how hard she tries."

I felt a chill run down my spine that had nothing to do with Donovan stroking the inside of my palm, and I shot a quick sideways glance to find—yep—there was Dmitri.

"Can you not?" I said to the spirit.

Donovan looked around for who I was talking to, then nodded. "Spirit?"

"Yep. Sorry. One sec." I returned my attention to the ghost. "I'm on a date."

"Exactly. And it looks like it's going well. You should break the news to him now."

"Not a chance."

"You said you would."

"Please, just... I'll talk to you later."

Dmitri disappeared and I turned to find Donovan looking a little less cheerful than before. "Another admirer?" he asked.

"What? Oh... No. Not like that at all."

"Would you tell me if it was?"

"Of course," I lied. "You knew about Roland."

"Only because he appeared out of thin air behind Sheehan's."

Good point. "Even still, you knew about him."

Light from the tea candle on the table between us danced across his features as he squinted at me. "Are there more?"

"More what?"

"More past-life boyfriends hunting you down."

I groaned. If he was insecure about *that*, just wait until he heard what else I had to tell him. "If there are, I don't know about them. Why are you so worried about it all of the sudden?"

He shrugged like it was no big deal, but he'd stopped stroking the inside of my palm. "Not worried. Just curious. After all, you kept me on the side for a long time while you were still with Tanner. How can I know that you don't have someone else on the side while you're with me?"

You bet your hide I yanked my hand out of his. "First of all, screw you. And second, you weren't 'on the side.' That makes it sound like I wasn't doing everything in my power to turn you down left and right."

"Whoa, whoa. I didn't mean to get you all riled up."

"Okay, fine. I can play this game, too. How do I know you're not currently trying to break up another one of your best friends' relationships to get his girl while we're together, like you were doing while you were with Eva?"

Rather than admitting I had an equally valid point, he leaned back in his chair and crossed his arms. "I wouldn't have done all that for anyone but you."

"Would you listen to yourself?" I grabbed the napkin off my lap and tossed it on the table. "It was Dmitri Flint. That's who just interrupted our date that was going *great* until you decided to accuse me of cheating on you with... what, *ghosts*? For fang's sake!"

Though it was clear I was about five seconds from leaving, Donovan didn't back down. "Dmitri was single. And it's been almost a week since he died. Why is he sticking around unless feelings for someone are keeping him here?" He raised his eyebrows like he'd just put me in checkmate.

"I love you, Donovan, but you're such an idiot." I stood and made for the exit.

"You— Hey, wait, Nora!"

I could hear his heavy footsteps behind me and had a perverse impulse to laugh. How many women had

Donovan been forced to chase after as they stormed out of Franco's Pizza? At least two that I knew of now, and that was just in the time since I'd been in Eastwind.

I was only a few yards out the door when I realized how insane I was being. How did this always happen with us? I wasn't usually emotional, but when it came to Donovan things could go from zero to sixty in a second flat.

This didn't have to happen. This night could still turn out just fine if I apologized and set my mind to making things better.

But the moment I turned around, we collided. His mouth was on mine in a heartbeat. I wove my fingers into his tangle of dark hair, pulling him closer. I was so tired of fighting, of these little things that tried to drive us apart. I didn't care about them anymore. I just wanted it to be the two of us. I wanted everything else in this world to leave us alone so we could have this all the time. No more suspicions, no more spirits, no more memories of the past.

He broke the kiss, his mouth a tantalizing inch from mine. "You said you love me in there. Did you mean it?"

I swallowed hard. Uh, had I really said that?

I replayed the moment in my mind. Yep, I had.

And had I really meant it in *that* way?

"I guess so," I said. "If I didn't, there's no way I would tolerate all your unicorn swirls."

"Goddess, Nora. I love—"

I touched a finger to his lips to stop him. "I know you do. You don't even have to say it. Because if you didn't love me, you would never put up with *my* unicorn swirls."

He kissed my finger and then took that hand in his.

"Nothing you ever do could drive me away. And Heaven knows you've tried."

Every atom in my body wanted to kiss him again then tell him to take me back to his place. Our night would no doubt unfold in a glorious tangle of warm skin and promises...

But it wasn't my atoms that ran the show, no matter how much things would have been different—perhaps better—if they did.

"There's something I have to tell you." The words were out before I could think twice. My Insight had forced them out, I was sure. Cursed Insight!

"Anything," he said, still holding my body against his. "Whatever it is, I don't care. So get on with it. The sooner you tell me, the sooner we can go back to my place." He hooked a finger underneath the neckline of my shirt, moving it to reveal more of my shoulder. "You have far too many clothes on."

Whoa, okay. I needed some space if I was going to get these words out. I stepped away from him, feeling my face rage with heat and not from the summer air. "I visited the count yesterday."

He tilted his head to the side, narrowing his eyes at me. "Okay?"

"I visited him in his castle, and he showed me something."

He continued to stare down at me, but now his dark brows pinched together. "O-kay...?"

Oh, just spit it out!

"There's a portal. He has a private portal."

Donovan's voice sounded weak as he asked, "Where does it lead?"

I could tell he already knew, but I spelled it out for him anyway. "My old world."

For a moment, his expression remained unchanged, and I thought this might not be as big of a deal as I'd made it out to be. He would react like a mature adult, remain calm, and explore my thoughts on the matter before jumping to any conclusions.

But then he collapsed into a cross-legged sit in the middle of the street, his hands falling limply into his lap. "Swirls."

I knelt in front of him, grabbing his shoulders. "I've already made my decision."

He nodded. "Yeah, you don't have to tell me. I guess part of me knew it couldn't last."

I shook him gently. "Goddess, you're an idiot." That snapped him out of it. "I made my decision to stay here. With you."

He hurried to his feet, pulling me up with him. "You're not going to look for him?"

"No." I paused. "Are you going to look for her?"

To his credit, he seemed to consider it before saying, "No."

"Then we're staying here." I leaned in and kissed him, and he returned it, though not as enthusiastically as I would have hoped. Okay, so maybe we wouldn't be sprinting off to his house, but perhaps we could still order our main entree and have an okay evening.

He stepped back. "It's not going to work, Nora."

"What?"

"When did you find out about it?"

"Yesterday. I've had time to sleep on it, and my decision hasn't changed."

He nodded. "You made the decision yesterday. And you're still here, so you made it again today. Maybe you'll even make the same one again tomorrow. But what about the day after that? With the portal there, you'll have to make the same decision every single day. And one of these days, you're going to miss him too much, and you won't choose me."

"You don't know that!"

"Then maybe I'll miss her too much and choose her!"

His flash of intensity caught me by surprise, and I took a quick step back. "Donovan, what are you saying?"

"I don't know. I just... How many days in a row will you choose me? Even one day of choosing him... it would break me, Nora. I was sorry about what happened to him, but I thought that maybe with time you'd be able to move on completely." He shook his head. "So long as that portal is open, you won't ever move on."

"Then we'll shut it!" I said. "We'll figure out how to close it and—"

"And what? Tell Sebastian Malavic that he has to let us? Not a chance. He would never do what we ask unless he thought it would cause us even more pain."

He was probably right about that. "Then we'll sneak in. Damnation, Donovan! I don't know what you want me to say! I'm staying here with you. I choose you!"

He closed the space between us, but only lifted one of my hands to his lips, kissing my palm. "I know. I just... It's a lot."

I remembered my reaction when I'd found out. "It is."

He let go of my hand. "I think I need some space to sleep on it."

"Are you breaking up with me?" The question sounded so lame, but it was out of my mouth before I could stop it.

"Never." He smiled softly, mournfully. "I'll never break up with you, Nora Ashcroft. If you want to get rid of me, you'll have to be the one to end it."

He tucked a piece of my hair behind my ear, rubbing his thumb over my cheek as he did, and then he turned and walked away.

I watched him go, his words swirling in my mind.

From behind me: "That went better than I thought it would."

I sighed and turned to face Dmitri. "Better than I thought it would, too... I think."

"Yeah, it was a bit confusing," he admitted. "Probably best not to think too hard about it tonight."

"What do you suggest instead? Alcohol?"

"No, no. There are other ways to self-medicate. Sleep is good. Pasta is better."

And so I took his advice and shuffled back into Franco's Pizza, one dead witch richer and one alive witch poorer.

Chapter Sixteen

The pasta did help, and so did the wine. Mostly the wine aided me in not giving two licks what people thought of me sitting at a table by myself, overindulging, and talking to someone no one else could see.

"I can already tell you won't let it go," he said. "You never will. That portal is literally an open door leading you back to him."

"You don't know anything," I said, noticeably slurring my speech. Whoops. "Okay, maybe you do. Maybe you're one hundred percent correct. So what?"

Dmitri was hovering in a sitting position on the chair where Donovan had been until, well, you know. "So, I think you did the right thing telling him."

"Shows what you know. Did you see his face? *I* did that to him." I gathered up a forkful of lasagna flotsam and shoveled it into my mouth, doing my best to talk around it. "I made him feel that way."

"I did see his face. And I've been in his shoes. It hurts. But it's necessary."

I went to wave down our server because it was half past tiramisu o'clock (yeah, dessert was happening), but paused and said, "What do you mean, you've been in his shoes?"

"Sasha Fontaine."

Tiramisu would have to wait. "Hold up. What?"

"Ansel's sister."

"I know who she is. But what do you mean that you— did you two have a thing?"

He nodded. "She was the one who got away."

"You mean when you were a kid? The one you commemorated with that tattoo?"

He nodded again.

"No," I said, "It's not the same thing."

He leaned forward so far parts of his chest disappeared into the edge of the table. "It's *exactly* the same." He leaned back again. "And I might have exaggerated with the kid thing. I was nineteen, and she was eighteen when it started. And Darius Pine was twenty."

"Darius Pine? What's he got to do with it? Actually, wait a second. I need dessert for this, *then* you can unload on me."

Once the order was in, I turned back to him again. "Okay, back in the game. What does Darius Pine have to do with this?"

"He was the other point in our love triangle. He stole her from me."

I narrowed my eyes at him. "Now, let's not start with that. She has a mind of her own. Maybe she just liked him better."

He chuckled. "You got me. Maybe so."

"So, which one were you?"

"What do you mean?"

I thanked our server as she dropped off the pick-me-up and I didn't hesitate to dive in after thanking her. "I mean, *obviously* I'm Sasha in this scenario. So are you Donovan or Tanner?"

"Donovan. Mostly."

"So you're telling me that Sasha was dating Darius, and then you and she performed a connection ritual that triggered a latent attraction that led to the two of you carrying on behind her boyfriend's back until she dropped you completely, and then Darius sprinted like an idiot through a portal, leaving you and her together finally, but then she found out that there was *another* portal and—"

"Not that direct of a correlation. And I was with her first."

"Oh."

"But I was too scared to make it official. I'd been in love with her since we were kids. My family used to rent a place on Fluke Mountain, and she lived in a cabin down the road. I only struck up the confidence to speak with her once we were older. It was actually Darius who officially introduced us at Lunasa Festival one year, and it went from there.

"We'd spent the whole day together, watching the Titan Games and the cook-off, and shopping. We might have stolen a little beer as well. I was in so deep, and I knew it. Spending a day with Sasha Fontaine was a dream come true. Then she told me: she'd had a crush on me since we were kids. I would have told her the same, but she kissed me behind one of the booths before I could. I grabbed her hand and we left together. Things were hot and heavy for a while, but we never had 'the talk.' I assumed it was obvious that I was in love with her. I was worried that if I started to say it, I would scare her away, that the depth of my feelings for her would be too much for an eighteen-year-old to bear.

"So we were just... friends, I guess. Officially, anyway."

I was already halfway done with my tiramisu by that point. "We call that friends with benefits where I come from."

"Makes sense. The benefits were many." He grinned. "But then things began to fall apart. We got into more fights than ever, and over stupid things. We got in a real blow-out about I-can't-even-remember-what, and I knew she would need some time to cool down. Usually, she'd come find me when she was ready, and we'd both apologize and make up. But this time, three days passed, and I still hadn't talked to her. I wasn't especially worried, until I saw her at Fulcrum Park. With Darius. They were lying on a blanket in the sun, clearly more cozy than two platonic friends would be.

"I interrupted their good time and asked her what was going on, what she was doing with *him*. She told me he was her boyfriend. I didn't know how long things had been going on between them, but I suspected longer than three days.

"And the worst part was that I couldn't argue with her. I couldn't say, 'But *I'm* your boyfriend!' because we'd never talked about that. I'd just assumed that she'd known, that it was obvious from the way we were carrying on. But, apparently, my lack of formality had only bred bitter resentment in her."

"Siren's song," I said, "she could have brought it up. It wasn't just to be up to you."

"That's true. But it doesn't excuse me from it."

I stared down forlornly at my now empty dessert plate. "I'm sorry that happened to you."

"It gets worse," he bemoaned. "She and Darius had their fair share of rough patches, and every time they did, guess who she came running to, just to talk things out."

"And did you? Talk things out, I mean?"

"At first, yes." And now a wry grin appeared on his face. "But one night, she showed up at my door with tears streaming down her face. She said she'd messed up, really crossed a line with him, and she was sure he would never take her back."

"What line did she cross?"

"I never found out."

"She wouldn't tell you?"

"She might have if I'd asked. But I wasn't thinking about that. All I was thinking was *Yes! Finally!* and she seemed to be thinking the same thing. We didn't do a whole lot of talking that night."

"So you two got back together?"

"No." He paused, staring in my direction but clearly focusing on something a thousand miles away. Spirits did that a lot. They love nostalgia. "That night was the last we had together. She said it was a mistake, blamed me for taking advantage of her when she was weak."

"Yikes." I could see her point, but I couldn't say I wouldn't have gone for it if I were in his shoes. "And she got back together with Darius?"

"No. She'd been right. She'd crossed a line, and they weren't getting back together."

I considered that a moment. "So, you and Darius both lost."

"Yes."

But both Dmitri and Darius were, from what I could tell, good men. Which meant Sasha had lost, too.

Everyone lost. Was that the way it went with love triangles? Was a loss across the board inevitable? Surely not.

I returned my attention to my wine, swirling the last portion at the bottom of the glass while my thoughts moved in much the same motion. Then I said, "And you're *sure* Darius wouldn't want to maul you to death?"

"Considering I'm dead, I'd say that ship has sailed."

I waved him off, hoping he would get on the same track as me without too much work on my part. "No, but I mean before you died."

"No, no, no. He and I straightened things out a few years later. Of course, it wasn't until *after* she married Paul Stormstruck. In fact, I'd say those turbulent years with her might have bonded Darius and me in a strange way."

"Paul Stormstruck... Is he the man she just divorced?"

"Well, he took her last name, so he was Paul Fontaine for a while, but yes. Same werebear."

I pondered it for a moment. "Do you think Donovan will give up on me?"

Without missing a beat, Dmitri answered, "Not a chance. He's braver than I was. He's never going to let you go so long as he has a breath in him. But he might respect it if you tell him to hold off."

"He did once. Sort of. I don't know if he would do it again."

"If you choose Tanner, he will. He loves you. Sure, he wants to be the one with you, but he also wants you to be happy. You have to pick who's right for you, not who you feel most sorry for."

"Donovan would hate Tanner forever if I went through that portal."

"No doubt. And it takes a lot for someone to hate Tanner Culpepper."

I nodded. Never a truer word spoken. Even Eastwind's crabbiest had a soft spot for him. And not for no reason. He'd been able to see the good in everyone, even those who the rest of the town turned their back on, and he treated people with respect.

Good goddess, he was a good man.

Is. He is a good man.

He was still alive somewhere. And now there was a way to get to him. So long as that existed, he wouldn't be past tense.

"Wait," I said, my mind catching up. "Did you know him?" I'd never considered the possibility, simply because *I* hadn't known Dmitri prior to his death. But Tanner knew most people in town.

"I knew him only casually. He was never at the Coven meetings. But I knew his parents very well. They *were* active in the Coven, and when they saw me getting into some darker stuff in my mid-teens, they stepped up and helped me out. I owe a lot to them. They took me under their wing when my own parents seemed set on pretending I didn't exist. And when they died..."

"Were murdered," I corrected. "By the High Priest."

He jerked his head back like I'd taken a swipe at him. "What?"

"Yep. I guess I can tell you, since you can't exactly go around telling everyone. Oh wait! Don't tell Ted."

"I won't. Why did he kill them?"

"It's a long story, but the gist of it is that it's my fault."

"You weren't even in Eastwind then."

"Like I said, it's a long story."

I reached for the wine bottle on the table to pour myself a refill but paused and grabbed my water glass instead. That's called being an adult.

"The Culpeppers were good people," Dmitri added. "And everything I heard and saw for myself about Tanner said the same."

"Yeah," I said, "A whole family of good people. And all gone."

"Not all gone." He held up a finger. "One is still around. And he doesn't know there's a way home."

"Then he can't miss what he doesn't know."

"But you can. And I think you do, Nora."

I groaned. "Of course I do! You think loss ever disappears? I loved him. Love him. But he left me, and now I love Donovan."

He cocked his head to the side. "You do?"

"Yes," I mumbled.

"Ah, I just thought you'd meant it casually and then decided to stand by the statement so he wouldn't storm off."

I threw my hands into the air. "Sphinx's riddle,

Dmitri! How much of our conversation did you listen to?"

"All of it. What? It was a good moment. Passionate in all the right ways."

"Except when he turned and left."

The spirit shrugged. "Call me crazy, but I think that might have been the most passionate part of the whole thing."

Chapter Seventeen

The Friday breakfast rush bled over into the Friday lunch rush, which didn't let up. Jane came in to take over for me and immediately found herself in the weeds, even while I stayed on a bit longer.

Finally, I had a chance to slip away into the manager's office and run over some of the sales for the morning, but my quiet time wasn't long lived. The bell at the back door rang loudly, announcing a letter. I went out to find that the owl had already departed, and the letter was waiting for me in the drop box below the perch.

I unrolled it and read: *MagEx at* 3:30. *Want you there. Stu.*

I popped back into the office to check the clock. It was 3:20. "Swirls!" As I grabbed up my things, patting my pockets to make sure I had my keys, Dmitri appeared.

"Where are you off to in such a hurry?"

"Gotta see the magical examiner. They're checking out your body at the sheriff's department today."

"Mind if I join?"

"As long as you don't make it weird, it seems like your right."

"Should I get Grim and Monster?"

"You can try, but I'd bet they'd both rather stick out the heat of the day indoors with the possibility of scraps than haul their hides into town. Heck, *I'd* rather do that, too."

We arrived just five minutes late. The sweat soaking through my shirt on my lower back and, regretfully, underneath my breasts, would at least show that I'd hurried over as quickly as I could.

"They're already down in the examination room," Jingo said, painting his toenails a vomit green at his desk. "You know how to get there."

I did.

When I arrived downstairs, the cellar coolness a welcome relief, I knocked on the glass, and Stu let me in. "Just in time, Ms. Ashcroft. I was worried you wouldn't be able to make it."

"Why? Because you only gave me 15 minutes' notice?"

He nodded. "Sorry about that."

Dmitri followed me in, and when he passed too close to the deputy, Stu said, "He's here?"

"Yep. Seemed only fair."

Magical Examiner Calvin Brightburn was a small witch with large, thick-rimmed glasses resting on a button nose that seemed ill-suited for an adult. He wore sky blue robes with the official Eastwind Coven crest on the front, which told me two things: first, he was probably a North Wind, and second, his allegiance was to the Coven over the sheriff.

Once we were set, the MagEx held his wand at both ends, closed his eyes, and held the stick just beyond Dmitri's feet, then began moving it slowly up toward Dmitri's head. I had no idea what he was looking for, but that was okay, because I wasn't the MagEx, so I didn't need to know.

They kept the body covered in a sheet, which was a small mercy, not just for me, but for Dmitri's spirit as well, I'm sure. The wand progressed over his knees, then his thighs, his hips, stomach, sternum—

"Huh," Brightburn said when the wand reached Dmitri's chest. "Deputy Manchester, could you pull back the coverings? There seems to be some kind of disturbance."

Stu pulled back the blanket just enough to expose the tattoo on Dmitri's chest.

"Very interesting," said the examiner, leaning over it. He poked it with the tip of his wand.

"Watch where you're sticking that thing," Dmitri said.

As Brightburn proceeded to draw little figure eights in the air above the Dmitri's heart with his wand, Stu Manchester explained, "The MedEx already concluded that it was a heart condition that ended his life. You'll find all that in the report."

The MagEx whipped his head around to glare at the deputy. "You think I haven't read the report? Of course I know what the MedEx said. But there's a reason there are two of us who examine every body, and this is a prime example of why the system exists."

"How do you mean?" I asked.

"I mean," Brightburn said impatiently, "the MedEx

was able to tell you that it was his heart that stopped. And you seem to believe he had a heart condition. But I'm here to tell you that the heart failure was, in fact, due to magic."

"Come again?" I said.

He waved a palm back and forth over Dmitri's tattoo. "There's a cord here."

"I don't see anything," said Stu.

"Of course you don't. It's not a visible cord. It's a magical one. It's more like a tether, really, because I can tell from the tension it's connected to something else. But I'm not sure what."

"What kind of energy are you getting from it?" Stu asked. "Dark? Light?"

"It's a curse," the examiner announced firmly. "I can't explain why, but I've felt enough of these to know. The curses hold on tight, and this one seems rather old."

"Do you think it's related to the tattoo?" I asked.

The MagEx looked at me like I should not have been let in the room, due to low intelligence. "Of course it is."

So there *was* more to the story of the mark than Dmitri had let on. I turned around to ask him more, but, somewhat predictably, he'd vanished.

Son of a banshee. He must have known he'd just been caught in a lie. Just an innocent tattoo? Not so much.

Oh well. He'd be back, and when he was, I'd anchor his haunted hide to the spot until I got some real answers.

As the examiner continued his investigation, jotting occasional notes in his report before running the wand back over various parts, Stu turned to me. "Looks like it might be a homicide after all." To his credit, it sounded like he was trying very hard not to gloat. But he wasn't doing a great job of it.

"You don't know that. If the mark has anything to do with the curse, well, he put that on himself as far as we know."

Stu's brows pinched together, and his mustache hitched to the side. "Why don't you just ask him?"

"He split."

"That's suspicious."

"No kidding."

Stu tucked his thumbs into his duty belt. "You think he cursed himself and it's what's keeping him here?"

"I'd be shocked if that wasn't the case, given what we just learned."

The deputy sighed. I knew he wasn't a huge fan of magic, possessing none himself outside of his ability to shift into an elk at will. I wasn't big on magic myself, so I understood. He said, "Did he ever tell you what that tattoo means?"

"He told me, but I think he might have been skewing the facts a bit. I'll have to follow up with him before I confirm anything. But I have a strong hunch."

Stu nodded. "That's good news. Your hunches are usually pretty solid."

I nodded my appreciation for his approval, and we left the MagEx to finish up his paperwork without us.

But what I didn't tell Stu, as we climbed out of the cool basement and into the main floor of the station, was that I had *more* than a hunch on this case now.

I had a theory.

And it involved Dmitri Flint, Sasha Fontaine, and Darius Pine.

Chapter Eighteen

Until Dmitri decided to stop hiding and start talking, there wasn't much I could do for the investigation other than, perhaps, try that meditation thing again. But I was so far from mastering that skill that it was laughable.

And I had a far more pressing matter to attend to after leaving the Sheriff's Department.

Since my dinner conversation with Dmitri the night before, all kinds of scenarios had spun their way through my mind. Did I know what I was going to do about the portal? Not quite. I had strong opinions about it, don't get me wrong, but I hadn't landed on anything definite.

What I *was* sure about was that I absolutely had to make things right with Donovan. I couldn't leave things the way they were.

I wasn't sure when his shift at Franco's started, but I knew it was sometime around now. His house was farther away than Franco's Pizza, so I decided to start at the latter.

I entered, and the hostess first greeted me like an old

friend then said, "Donovan's already behind the bar, if that's who you're looking for."

I suspected that under normal circumstances she wouldn't have tacked on the "if that's who you're looking for," but that my tipsy dinner date with a ghost had muddied the waters a bit.

I thanked her and stepped into the dining area. The second my eyes found him, my heart skipped a beat. I wanted to stay and watch him for a while longer. His family turned up their noses at his chosen profession, but bartending was what he enjoyed, and he was great at it. And that was more than what most people could say about their careers.

He flicked his wand, and bottles poured themselves into glasses of various sizes, whizzing either to customers seated at the bar or drink trays that the servers could grab and go.

And when his eyes locked onto mine, everything hovered in place for a quick second, and I was subjected to that sharp look from him I knew all too well—it was the one I'd seen in all those encounters before our first adventure into the Deadwoods. But what did it mean now, after so much had happened?

The objects in the air finished their movements, landing effortlessly where they belonged, but no more jumped off the shelves. A waiting customer tried to order a drink, but Donovan held up a finger for him to wait one second, and then he nodded for me to follow him to the kitchen.

Silently, I complied, and he didn't say a word to me until we were in the narrow back alley.

"Donovan, I know you're still upset, but I just want

to say—" I didn't get to finish before his body pressed mine against the wall and he silenced me with his lips.

How many times? I wondered. How many times would we have passionate moments in back alleys?

A thousand times wouldn't be enough. Making out with Donovan in shady back alleys felt exactly like the type of romance we'd been building since day one.

My heart raced as I let his hands roam. Mine roamed as well, undoing the top few buttons of his shirt.

"Damnation, Nora," he breathed in my ear, "I need you so bad. I don't care if it only lasts another day. I'll take whatever you'll give me."

I moaned as his teeth found nape of my neck. I undid another button and ran my hands over the blazing hot skin of his chest. And when the palm of my hand found his heartbeat, the connection came thundering back. The bookshelf.

I yanked my hand away like I'd been scalded, and he gave my shoulder a break long enough to cast me a concerned glance. "Did I hurt you? Sorry. I got a little carried away. I just—"

"No," I assured him. "I just remembered something."

"You just... remembered something?" His chest was heaving, and I knew the confusion that held back another flood of passion was tenuous at best.

"Yes." I frowned and shook my head. "Sorry, sorry. It's just that Dmitri has this tattoo over his heart, and the magical examiner said the symbol was attached to a curse. And I *knew* I'd seen that symbol before, but I couldn't remember where."

"And you just remembered," he said, sounding not nearly as excited by the idea as I was.

"I did. And I should probably..."

"Go," he said, taking a step back. "Right." He cleared his throat and began the arduous task of buttoning up his shirt.

"Sorry," I said. "I just... If it's what I think it is, it's seriously dark magic, and the sooner I can clean it up the better."

"Will you come back?"

I couldn't quite decipher his pained expression. "You mean, to Franco's?

"No, to me."

My heart filled with lead. "Of course. Donovan, I already told you I'm not going anywhere."

He nodded then turned to lean his back against the wall next to me. "I thought you'd have already left by now. I thought when I walked away, you would take it as a sign that you were better off without me."

I turned my head to look at him. "Were you trying to run me off?"

He met my stare. "Of course not. I already told you I wouldn't leave. But let's not kid ourselves, we both know it's only a matter of time before I do something to drive you away for good."

"Hey," I whispered, placing a palm on his jaw. "If you could do something to push me away, don't you think I'd already be gone?"

He narrowed his eyes at me. "It kind of sounds like you're saying I'm hard to be around."

"You are." I pushed off the wall, moved to stand in front of him, and kissed him softly on the lips. "But you always make up for it later."

And then I turned and left. I needed to get some

distance from him. Not just for the sake of public decency, but because I'd never felt so torn in all my life.

I could never leave Donovan, could I? It wasn't that I wanted to, but even if I *had* wanted to, I couldn't now. He was so vulnerable.

And sexy. So very sexy.

But as I passed Fulcrum Fountain on my way to Erin Park, I had the strangest sensation. It was like the open portal was hovering just a few feet behind me, following my every step, and calling for me to turn around and take the leap.

Chapter Nineteen

"I promise I wasn't watching," were the first words out of Dmitri's mouth when he appeared a moment later.

"Voyeur," I mumbled. "If you weren't watching, how did you know it was happening?"

"Okay, so I caught the tail end of it, but I didn't mean to. I gotta tell you, Nora, you're in deep with that guy."

I glared at him. "You're in deep, too. In deep swirls. How come you didn't tell me the truth about the tattoo?" I continued stomping toward Greggory O'Leary's house as he drifted after me.

"What do you mean?"

"It's a curse!"

"Oh, right. That."

"You didn't think it was worth mentioning that the tattoo over your *failed* heart, which we just discovered was tethering you magically to something in the physical world, was a result of a curse? And a dark leprechaun curse, if I'm not mistaken. Everyone knows their curses are the most unforgiving."

He cringe-grinned. "It didn't seem relevant."

I came to a halt and rounded on him. "It didn't seem relevant? Did you, by any chance, find out about your mysterious heart condition *after* you tattooed yourself?"

"Yes, but—"

"I want the real story, Dmitri. Stop wasting my time. I'm trying to help you move on!"

He opened his mouth, and through it I noticed an owl swooping out of the night sky to land on a mail perch and ring the bell.

Finally, he said. "That night, when Sasha came over and said she was done with Darius for good, I wanted to believe it. Not just for my sake, but for hers. I wanted her to be able to move on from him."

"You can drop that act," I snapped. "Remember who you're talking to. You don't have to pretend your actions were based on anything other than selfish and poor decisions. I know how it goes. I'm practically the *queen* of that when it comes to romance." Maybe I was being a little hard on myself, but hey, it felt great.

"Fine," he said. "I wanted to make sure they never made up because I was so tired of being second place. I wanted to be her first choice. And after that night at my place, the thought of them ever getting back together nearly tore my heart out. So, once she left, I took action."

"What do you mean? The curse?"

"Yes. I went over to Greggory's and asked him to help me with a ritual. When I told him what it was, he flat out refused. He said messing with love magic was more than he had a stomach for. It was one thing to cast a confusion charm on someone so we could swipe a little booze from behind the bar at Sheehan's, but it was another to set this degree of curse against another person.

"I didn't understand the concept of permanence at the time. I was nineteen! Forever seemed like both a long and a short time to me. I couldn't even think two days ahead of me, let alone two or twenty years. So, on my way out of his house, I swiped one of his books."

I nodded along. "The one with that symbol on the spine."

His eyebrows shot up. "You've seen it?"

"When I went to speak with him. I'd glanced at his bookshelf, but the symbol meant nothing to me at the time. It just now came back to me."

"And that's why you're marching over to knock down his door, huh?"

"Precisely."

"He didn't have anything to do with it. It was all me. I took the book, returned home, and performed the curse myself. Then I returned it to him before he knew it was gone. It was almost a year before he learned what I'd done. And you should know he took me outside and kicked my hide for it."

"I'm not going to shout at him," I said, starting back on my route. "I'm just going to get the book. If you're ever going to move on, we have to lift this curse."

He was silent for a moment, then said, "Makes sense."

I knew I should detach myself from this situation. After all, it was work, but for fang's sake, I'd come to like him, and even though I knew not to trust spirits at their word, his lies and obscuring of the truth ate at me. So I had to ask him: "Did you know this was what was keeping you the whole time?"

"No. I honestly didn't. That's the truth! I never read up on the consequences of the spell. I was an idiot at the time, like I said. And then within a few years, I'd forgiven both Sasha and Darius, and I figured that was the end of it. Sure, the tattoo was still there but as far as I was concerned, it was just a reminder of how quickly the grudges that we think will last forever can fade. I really don't have any unfinished business with them."

"Except you do. Whatever this curse is made of, it's powerful stuff, and it's anchoring you here until it's lifted."

I was tempted to accept his answer as truth, though. Would I be a fool to believe this when he'd omitted so much in the past to spare his own ego?

We reached O'Leary's home, walked up onto the stoop, but before I knocked, Dmitri said, "What will you do once I'm gone?"

His question caught me by surprise. "The same thing I've always done, probably."

"No, I mean regarding Donovan and Tanner. What will you do?"

"I promised Donovan I would stick around."

"So, what, you're going to stay with him until Ted do you part because you made a promise under duress? What about making yourself happy?"

I hissed, "You think I can't be happy with Donovan?"

"Not while you know Tanner is out there, just a portal away."

"Except he won't be." Amid the chaos of the last

twenty minutes, something had shifted inside me, and the best answer to my problems had become clear, solidifying in my mind. "Because I'm going to close the portal."

Dmitri looked at me with something not unlike pity. "You think you're going to ask the count to close it and... he will?"

"No. I know he won't."

"Then you're planning on breaking into his castle to close it?"

"Of course not."

"Then how are you going to close it?"

"I don't know yet, *okay*?"

The door swung open suddenly, and light from the lamp in Greggory O'Leary's hand temporarily blinded me.

"Fangs and claws," I hissed, covering my eyes.

"I should've known it was you out here talking to no one on my doorstep," the leprechaun said, lowering the lamp. "Or are ya talking to someone I just can't see?" When my vision returned to me, I noted that he was wearing a heather-green bath robe and a fuzzy orange nightcap that hung limply over his right ear. If it was already past dusk, it was only just. Going to bed this early seemed strange, but, well, who was I to judge? I was arguing with a ghost on his doorstep.

"Someone you can't see."

"Dmitri?"

"Yep."

O'Leary turned and motioned for us to follow him inside, and I shut the door behind us.

He set the lamp on the table and then proceeded to

light a few of the candles in the sconces protruding from his mossy walls.

"Vision's not what it used to be," he said. "Practicing too much Draíolc in your impressionable years can do that. Dims the light. I can see all right when it's a bright day, but outside of that... It's too bad how that works, that life convinces us we're immortal and that our bill will never come due when we're young, and then it comes due over and over again, with interest added. Shall I make some tea?"

"I'd prefer whiskey."

He nodded and winked. "Right answer."

He grabbed a bottle and two clay cups from a shelf next to his bookcase and brought them over.

I downed the first bit quickly, and he poured me a refill. "What's this about?"

I stood and moved over to his books. "This, actually." Locating the symbol on the spine, I pulled it out to show him. "What's this one about?"

"Curses."

"Specifically?"

"Love curses. The most dangerous kind there is."

I knew better than to question that assertion. I'd seen firsthand the kind of chaos that could erupt from love run amok when Cassie the Archetype decided to drop into Eastwind and stir up old romances. Ansel was lucky not to be in Ironhelm after what he'd done during the frenzy.

"And the one on the spine?"

"Ah, so yer putting it all together, then. That's the Lamora Knot. Easily the most recognizable but also the most misunderstood and dangerous symbol of this variety."

I stared down at it. "Then why would anyone put it on the cover? Seems a bit reckless."

"It is." He shrugged. "But it's kinda pretty, innit?"

I sighed. "Yeah, I guess so." Setting it on the table in front of Dmitri with a *thump*, I said, "Now we just have to figure out how to break the knot."

Chapter Twenty

The book of Draíolc spells hadn't revealed the counter-curse for the Lamora Knot without a good fight. But in the end, O'Leary's magical know-how had won out, and through a series of chants and spells, he'd convinced the old book to reveal the cure. The page where the instructions for the curse had once been had changed *reluctantly*—I cannot stress that enough, though describing how I could tell a piece of paper was reluctant is beyond my ability to explain—to a description of what needed to be done to undo the damage. I wasn't especially fond of the answer, but I'd worry about that bit of unpleasantness when the time came.

Once that bit of work was done, I translated for Dmitri as he bid his best friend a final goodbye in O'Leary's parlor. It wasn't the kind of heartfelt goodbye I'd gotten used to delivering for spirits. Instead, it was little more than an inventory list of all the places throughout Eastwind where Dmitri had buried various items of their stolen contraband over the years. He gave

O'Leary his blessing to dig up whatever he saw fit to sell in the event the leprechaun ever found himself hard up for cash. At O'Leary's insistence, I promised not to tell anyone what I'd just learned. The man—bathrobe, nightcap, and all—looked about ready to make me swear a blood oath, and I bet he knew a few good ones.

But in the end, he took me at my word, and Dmitri and I stepped out into the fading twilight.

"Wait," he said.

I turned around just in time to see him scurry out of sight, leaving the front door open. He appeared again a moment later, carrying something long in his hand. He offered it to me, and, at first, I wasn't sure what it was. Then it sank in.

"What's this for?" I asked, receiving the dagger. The scabbard was a thick, stiff, woven leather tinted dark green, and a smooth bronze hilt jutted out from the sheath.

"Completing the ritual. Cutting this kind of knot requires the right kind of knife. I suspect the sheriff will want to confiscate it after ya use it, so do whatever ya need to get it back to me. It's worth more than all of Flint's buried knickknacks combined."

I agreed to do my best and tucked it in my waistband before saying a final farewell to Greggory O'Leary.

And then I made for Fluke Mountain.

"You could just send him a letter, you know. That's what owls are for," Dmitri said, floating alongside.

"We're not going to visit Darius yet. We can deal with that in the morning."

"Then where are we going?"

"You'll see."

"I'm afraid my energy is almost tapped."

"Then it's time to dig down deep. You're not done yet."

Twenty minutes later, we finally turned a corner on a narrow foot path and her cabin came into sight.

Our real purpose for the trek hit him. "No," he said. "No, no, no. This is totally unnecessary."

"You have to shut the door on this, Dmitri. And I could tell from the way you talked about her that it's still open *at least* a crack."

He wrung his ghostly hands, and I noticed one fade out of existence for a moment. He wasn't kidding about his energy being low. "But what am I even going to say?"

I reached in my back pocket and pulled out a pen and a piece of owl parchment I'd stolen from O'Leary's house.

What? The man spent the first part of his life being a petty criminal! Losing a pen and some paper to me was the least of his karma.

"When you're ready, you can use me to write it."

He stared at me, aghast. "*Use* you?"

"Yep." I reached in my shirt and pulled out the staurolite pendant, removing the chain from around my neck. "I'm all yours. You can even use my energy."

He squinted at me through the gloom. "You mean... possess you?"

"Yep."

"You trust me to do that?"

"It's probably a grave error in judgment, but yes."

"Huh. Well, thanks. I appreciate that. I didn't figure you would, after everything."

As I looked around for a good place to sit, I said, "I

don't trust you to tell me everything you know, but do I think you're going to possess me and never let me go? Or make me run off some cliff? No."

"I don't know how to do it."

I settled onto a large boulder and placed the slip of paper on my thigh. "You'll figure it out. Your kind are naturals at it."

He did figure it out, and as he wrote his final letter to Sasha Fontaine, I kept my mind to myself and didn't read a word of it. He made me fold it up and then slipped it in my pocket before releasing his hold on me. Not that I had *any* desire to read it. Snooping on that sort of an intimate moment felt, well, I don't have a word to describe it other than *icky*.

I looped my pendant back over my head and nodded. "Okay, ready?"

"I am. One question, though. How did you know Sasha's address?"

We stepped onto her porch, and I'm proud to say I'd learned my lesson about carrying on loudly on doorsteps from our last stop; this time I was quieter when I said, "I employ her daughter. I see this address on her payment slip each week."

It was a long moment after I knocked before the door opened, but it wasn't Sasha staring back at me. It was Greta. "What are *you* doing here?" she asked with the unintentional and omnipresent rudeness of teenage girls that I secretly loved. Then her eyes grew large. "Oh no, am I fired?"

"No. Should you be?"

She shook her head without taking her eyes off me.

"Definitely not. My mom makes me buy all my own books at Mancer Academy. I need this job."

"Great. Then we're on the same page. Speaking of your mom, is she home?"

She merely nodded once before hollering over her shoulder, "Mom! Nora Ashcroft wants to talk to you."

Sasha, who looked well on her way with winding down for the night, pulled a silk robe closer to her around her nightgown as she appeared in the living room a moment later. Greta wandered off without another word.

"What can I help you with?" she said. Then quickly, "Is everything okay?"

I knew that look of alarm all too well. But to be fair, I did sort of run with Death. "Everything's fine. I just wanted to give you something." I reached in my pocket and pulled out the letter. "It's from Dmitri." I handed it to her and said, "Don't read it now."

Did I want to spare her the embarrassment of emotions in front of me? Why, of course. I can be sensitive and thoughtful when I try.

But mostly, I didn't think I could handle seeing her break down. It'd been a long day, and it was everything I could do not to have a good cry myself. And because there wasn't any time blocked for it in my schedule for the rest of that endless day, it would have to wait.

She nodded but peeked at a corner anyway. It must have been the sight of his handwriting that dredged up the emotion and brought moisture to her eyes. "You spoke with him?"

"Yes."

He said, "Tell her I'm here."

I ignored him.

"Will you speak with him again?"

"I will."

"Tell him I'm sorry. It always should have been him. I was just so hurt that he never... I was hurt and I wanted to hurt him."

I stuck my hands deep into my pants pockets. "Yeah, love can be like that."

"I'm sorry," she said, sniffing and running a finger under each eyelid to wipe away the spillover. "I haven't been the nicest to you. I shouldn't have made Greta quit. She loves that job, and you've been nothing but nice to her."

Yikes. I cannot tell you how much I didn't want to do this right then. "Don't worry about it," I said. "No one trusts me. Heck, I don't even trust myself, a lot of the time."

She nodded, and her eyes returned to the letter. "Tell him I always loved him."

Now, I should pause here to say that I only *assumed* what Dmitri wrote in his letter was something lovely and sentimental. For all I knew, he could have told her to drop dead. He never told me. I hoped it was nothing like that, but you never know.

"I think he knows," I said. "But I'll tell him."

He stood silently beside me, not saying a word, only staring at her for the last time.

"We'll let you get some sleep then," I said.

"We?"

Swirls.

"Uh, yeah. Sorry. Me and Grim. He's just sort of, um, lurking in the shadows."

"Ah okay."

"Take care of yourself, Sasha."

* * *

Dmitri said he needed some time to recharge, and I didn't fight him on it as I climbed the stairs up to my room. The door was open, and Monster and Grim were already snoozing on his dog bed. But my tired and clumsy footsteps on the baseboards woke them.

"Where've you been?"

"I don't even know where to start. Can we just talk about it in the morning? It's been a long day."

"Monster wants me to tell you that you should take her with you when you go through the portal."

"I'm not going through the portal."

"I told her you'd say that."

"You did?"

"I did. I also told her it didn't mean anything. You'll be going through that portal one way or another."

And now I switched to our silent connection for a little privacy from the feline eavesdropper. *"I'm not going through it. But I am going to close it. And I might need your help."*

"You mean my protection. From Malavic."

"Precisely. But like I said, let's just talk about this in the morning. I got nothing left tonight."

I slipped into my pj's—always a little weird with Grim around even though he seemed to be totally uninterested in my naked form, being perpetually naked himself—and then crawled into bed.

My head hitting the pillow was like the starting gun of a relay race. My mind sprinted at full speed, passing the baton between conundrums. I squeezed my eyes tight, but that didn't help. I resigned myself to a maddening sleepless night filled with swirling images of Donovan kissing me behind Franco's, Sasha's teary eyes, Dmitri's dead body, and—seared into my psyche for all eternity—my last glimpse of Tanner rushing after Eva right as the portal in the Deadwoods shrank to a pinprick and disappeared.

How much time had passed, ten minutes? Three hours? Something heavy caused the mattress to dip, and while it pulled me from my spiraling thoughts, I didn't have to open my eyes to know what it was. The shifting weight of giant paws moved farther up the bed before plopping down on my legs. Grim's breath whooshed out of him in a small grunt as he flopped. And a moment later, tiny, featherlight feet tugged the quilt tight as Monster crept to curl up against my chest.

They were brazenly violating our agreed-upon sleeping arrangements.

But they were so snuggly...

So I pretended to already be asleep. And then, a moment later, I was.

Chapter Twenty-One

I took the following day off from work, just called Bryant first thing and offered to pay him an entire gold coin to cover for me. Since I was his boss, I could have paid him nothing and just told him to do it, and he'd have had to. But that would have caused problems later, so it was worth it to pay him off for his trouble.

It should have felt great, having a day away from the demands and complaints of Medium Rare customers. Random days off were some of my favorite. The world was my oyster and whatnot! But not on this day. If anything, the world was feeling a little like one of those oysters that kills you within forty-eight hours of eating it.

It was a mild summer morning and would have been quite lovely in another context. The sky was powder blue with occasional cotton ball clouds wafting across. Sunflowers were in full bloom along the sides of the road, and birds chirped and swooped from tree to tree.

And I was on my way to ceremoniously remove a hunk of my newest friend's flesh.

Dmitri, who walked beside me, didn't seem put off by what was required in the ritual. The time alone to recharge had apparently helped him process his last interaction with Sasha, and there was a little extra pep in his float.

Grim padded along on the other side of me, holding himself rather stiffly and awkwardly. The illicit snuggling must have given him a crick in his back.

I turned to Dmitri. "You're not anxious at all?"

He pouted his lips and shrugged. "No. Why would I be?"

I hated to even bring it up if he wasn't already considering it, but my curiosity was too far ahead of me. "Because you don't know what's next. Once the knot is cut, you move on."

"Right. That's how it goes, I'm told. Do *you* know what's next?"

I wished I did. But at the same time, I was glad I didn't. "I've only heard bits and pieces, so I don't know with certainty. Although, based on personal experience, I do recommend against lingering in the in-between place to track down a lover from a past life when she enters the next life. It's just not worth it."

His mouth hung open slightly, and he arched an eyebrow at me. "You've done that?"

"No, but I've been the former lover on the receiving end of it. And that level of stalking is simply unrivaled, let me tell you."

He laughed, and I knew instantly I would miss the sound once it was gone. "You must have been a goddess in a past life."

I cringed. "I can tell you with some certainty that I was not. At least not in any of the last five."

"Then farther back than that. It's the only possible explanation."

"For what?"

"Maybe you were a goddess of love or lust or obsession, and *that's* why you have more men chasing after you than you can handle."

"Ulch," I said, "gag me. No, the more likely explanation is that I make poor romantic choices."

He nodded solemnly. "Yeah, that makes sense, too."

We entered the cool air of the sheriff's department where the rest of our group were already waiting. Stu Manchester was chatting in low tones with Sheriff Bloom and Jingo, and Darius Pine was sitting on one of the flimsy benches in the waiting area, running a hand back and forth over his hair while staring vaguely at the floor.

The sound of Grim and I entering caught their attention, and Bloom glided forward to greet us. "Good. You brought him, didn't you?"

"Seemed fair to let him come."

"And he won't try to stop it?"

"No, he's ready to move on to the next thing."

She nodded. "He may change his mind, and if he does, I'll expect you to handle it so we can complete the ceremony."

"Sheesh," Dmitri said, "what's a guy gotta do to get a little trust around here?"

From the side of my mouth, I mumbled, "Not cast dark leprechaun curses on Darius Pine, apparently."

He rolled his eyes. "One time. I only did it one time."

I couldn't help but chuckle at that. I hated that I

hadn't known him in life, but that was how it went sometimes. Things didn't work out the way you wanted them to, and everything was a little sad.

And, to be honest, I was worried about what would happen once we untethered him. Where would he go, and would it be pleasant?

The questions could be endless if I let them. And I was starting to believe that was for a clear purpose. Uncertainty can be healthy sometimes.

Bloom led us down to where Dmitri's body was laid out in the examination room.

Grim yelped just before we entered the room, and I whirled around to check on him. His tail was between his legs and he hung his head. *"Just a side stitch. Must have slept wrong."*

"Is he okay?" Darius asked. He seemed anxious, on edge, and it was clear from his expression that Grim's sudden noise was more than unwelcome while his nerves were in such a state.

"Yeah. I think he just slept funny last night. He says he's fine." I suggested Grim wait outside of the exam room, and he agreed without argument.

Our group gathered around the body on the table, and Bloom did the honors of pulling down the sheet just far enough to expose the tattoo. He didn't look any the worse for the time that had passed, and holy shifter was I glad for that small mercy. This was already going to be unpleasant, and adding a decomposing body to it wouldn't have made it any better.

And then they all looked at me.

Oh right. I was the only one who knew the ritual, aside from the ghost no one else could see.

I reached in my waistband where I'd tucked the ritual dagger O'Leary had loaned me the night before. I unsheathed it and offered it to Darius. "The curse is attached to you, so you have to do the cutting."

"The... cutting?" His tan face now held a hint of green. For the head of a werebear sleuth, he sure was squeamish.

"Yeah. I'll explain as we go."

He nodded and took the dagger. "And this... you're sure this is the reason I've had such poor luck in romance?"

"It's definitely a large part of it."

"And once we sever this cord, I won't keep messing everything up with women?"

"I can't promise you that. I mean, you still have to be nice and interesting. But you won't have a curse holding you back. If you bomb, it's all on you."

Darius Pine nodded and then said, "What do I do?"

I told him, step-by-step, before he began, but I didn't mention the last step—the one involving the dagger—which I thought might keep him from ever getting started. I handed him the slip of paper with the incantation written on it. Werebears weren't magical practitioners by nature, but anyone, given the right spells and tools, could do something like this.

"Any questions?" I asked.

"No." He moved forward and slashed the dagger through the air between his heart and Dmitri's, once, twice, thrice. Then began reading the words slowly and deliberately from the sheet of paper.

As he did, I glanced at the spirit of the deceased,

trying to get a read on his expression. His eyes were glued to his own face.

"What is it?" I asked him.

Dmitri frowned. "I just want to remember what I looked like. Maybe that's vain, but I want to remember myself, even after I move on. I don't want to lose everything I've learned and experienced in this life. I don't want my memory to fade into nothingness."

I didn't know what to say. I wanted to assure him it wouldn't, but I had a feeling it would, especially once he moved onto another life. And, strangely enough, I suspected that the oblivion was the greatest mercy we could ever experience, to forget ourselves completely, to lose our sense of self—our vanity, identity, ego, superego —and simply become nothing. And everything. At least until it was our time to start all over again. To start fresh.

"We'll remember you," I said. "*I'll* remember you. Even if you forget yourself, I'll remember who you are. That's what friends do."

Darius finished reciting the words looked up from the paper. "Okay, is that it?"

"Not yet," I said, readying myself to explain the last nasty bit. "There's one more step."

"And that is?"

"The dagger. You have to cut the mark out of him."

Darius's face twisted into disgust. "And do *what* with it?"

"Burn it. Cutting it out sends him on his way, and burning it closes the door behind him. The book said he can never return after that."

I sensed Darius's hesitancy deep inside my chest. It

was the typical energy people gave off when suddenly facing the concept of forever.

"Don't worry," I said. "It's doing him a favor."

Cringing, Darius leaned over the corpse and pressed the blade against skin.

I'll spare you the details. Mostly because I didn't see them. I had no desire to watch, and besides, Dmitri pulled my attention away from it.

"Thanks," he said. "I owe you one."

"After all your advice, which, yes, I did actually listen to, I think we're even."

"Will you look after Sasha?"

"I don't think I'll have to." I nodded at Darius, who was focusing so hard on his task that his tongue stuck out between his lips.

"That guy?" Dmitri said. "You think *he* can take care of her?" He sighed, and his form began fading fast. "I guess I'll just have to trust him."

"I'll make sure he doesn't do anything too stupid."

"I guess that's all I can ask for. Especially considering it was my own stupidity that got us in this mess."

"Don't take it so hard."

"Why not? It won't be for long."

Dmitri was hardly more than a mirage then. Darius was almost done.

"Happy trails," I said awkwardly. Not my usual go-to farewell, but it just came out. What? This was a strange situation, even for a psychic. I was off my game.

Dmitri's voice fluttered out as hardly more than a whisper. "Happy trails?"

"It's just a thing we use to say in my own world. It means, um, have a good ride."

And then I heard his pleasant chuckle for the very last time. "I like it. Happy trails to you, Nora."

And then Dmitri Flint, East Wind witch and my newest friend, disappeared.

Forever.

"Do I have to... touch it?" came Darius's voice.

I turned back toward the body, the grisly scene hitting me like a bucket of cold water. I crinkled up my nose. "I don't think so."

Bloom instructed Stu to grab some gloves and a small evidence bag, and the deputy hustled over to a small table and returned with the goods. And a few seconds later, it was, as they say, all over but the crying.

And, you know, burning the flesh. But I had no intention of being present for that.

Going from the cold chill of the exam room out into the hot summer air felt like a fever breaking. Or maybe it was saying goodbye to Dmitri that made me feel that way.

Darius stood next to me on the top step of the stairs leading up to the building. He held a small metal biscuit tin in which we'd tucked away the gory talisman (it was the only suitable container we could find for the baggie so he wouldn't have to look at it). Neither us nor Grim made to leave yet. "So, I just burn it?" asked the werebear.

"Yeah. Burn it and... maybe spread his ashes in some of his old haunts. Outside Sheehan's Pub, Rainbow Falls, Fluke Mountain. Places from his life where we can remember him, where people can visit if they want."

He nodded, and I saw his eyes grow red.

"He didn't mean to do it," I said. Then I quickly added, "Well, at first he did. Definitely. But he didn't know the curse was still around once the two of you made right."

"Yeah, I figured as much. He was the kind of guy who let you know if he didn't like you. And I could tell we were actually friends."

"I'm glad you remember him that way. And do me a favor," I added. "Don't finish this process alone."

He appeared suddenly hopeful. "You'll do it with me?"

"Oh, hellhound no! Not a chance." I reeled it back in. No point in reminding him how unpleasant the rest of the counter-curse would be. "Maybe see if Sasha will do it with you."

He jerked his head back. "Sasha? Like, Ansel's Sasha?"

"Or your Sasha, yeah. Her."

He immediately looked away, taking in the view from where we stood. "She won't want to do it. Not with me."

"I have reason to believe she might want to remember him, too."

Again, this was me *assuming* the letter from Dmitri hadn't explicitly told her to eat a pile of dragon dung.

Darius sighed, his bulky shoulder deflating. "Well, when *you* have reason to believe something, I find it's better not to ask what that reason is, and just to do it."

"I wish there were more people like you in Eastwind." I stepped closer and put my arm around him, initiating a side hug.

But before I could pull away, I found myself wrapped up tight in the werebear's thick arms. "Thanks," he said into my hair. "And if you ever tell anyone you saw me emotional, we will no longer be friends."

"Got it," I muttered into his left pec.

He released me and then we parted ways—he headed straight for Fluke Mountain, and Grim and I made for our next rallying point to finish up the last bit of insanity I had left in my day off work...

Chapter Twenty-Two

Grim lagged behind, the poor guy's gait looking even more off-kilter than before, while Donovan and I strolled toward Widow Lake to pay a little surprise visit to Eastwind's most lovable and only vampire.

Donovan wasn't totally sold on my game plan, though. "We just tell him we want to go through the portal, and then we shut it?"

"Yeah, how is that so hard?"

"Uh, do you know how to shut a portal?"

I waved my hand vaguely. "I have an idea of how it works... sort of."

He groaned. "What does that mean?"

"It means I read up on it."

"You *read up on it*? When?"

I felt slightly guilty as I answered, "At the end of last year. I might have spent a little bit of time in the library researching how to open one."

He didn't seem bothered by the new information, though. "And it said how to close them, too?"

"Maybe? But I didn't see the point in learning how to close one until I learned how to open one."

The number of passersby thinned as we reached the outer rings of the town proper. Donovan said, "I take it you never learned how to open one, did you?"

"No, I never did figure it out. But I learned a lot about the concepts."

He sighed and his head drooped. "And you think that's enough to—"

"It's your fault I stopped!" I snapped. "You distracted me with all that New Year's Eve talk of new beginnings, and I figured life might be better without any portals at all."

"Considering what we're on our way to do, I couldn't agree with that sentiment more."

"And that's why we're doing this. To carry on portal-free!"

"Except for the one to Avalon."

I nodded. "And the one through the tree tunnel in the Deadwoods."

"Ah yes. Can't forget that one, can we?" he said, sliding an arm around my waist. "Why don't we just take a little trip into the Deadwoods right now? We could practice our portal-closing techniques on that one first."

It wasn't a bad idea, all lethal threat of the Deadwoods aside.

"Maybe I want to leave that one open," I said.

"Why's that?"

"I have pretty good memories of that cliff's edge. I might want to revisit it."

He groaned softly and stepped in front of me, putting his lips to mine.

I was lying, of course. I had zero desire to return to the place where a drought demon possessed me, the place where Donovan almost died, and where the pungent scent of Grim's urine still undoubtedly haunts the nostrils of all who dwell there.

PTSD anyone? A little making out with Donovan there wouldn't undo that.

But his suggestion did raise a good question. Why *was* I rushing into this before I was completely ready?

The smart thing to do would be to take Donovan back to the library with me and enlist his help finding out how to close a portal. Bonus points for figuring out what sort of ramifications might go along with closing a portal after nature had already balanced itself.

But I was anxious. No, that word wasn't strong enough for what I felt. Every fiber of my being felt like it would grow legs and run off in a different direction if I waited another day to make this decision. Or worse, I wouldn't choose this option at all. I would pick another one. The one a large part of me had wanted to make since Malavic revealed the gateway to me.

Images of me walking through the portal and being reunited with Tanner had been flashing in my mind at odd times over the last couple of days, challenging my resolve.

And shutting the door behind Dmitri had been a thing of relief, even if it was also painful. It was ripping off a band-aid, a moment of intense pain that fades surprisingly fast, and you know you're better off having gone through it.

I wanted that. Closing the portal and saying goodbye to both Eva and Tanner would be the hardest thing I'd ever done. It would hurt so terribly—I could already imagine the nausea, the dizziness—but I would have Donovan with me, and it would pass. The painful sore wouldn't continue to fester. I would lance it and move on.

Was I concerned we couldn't shut the portal?

Oddly, no. Because I had faith in my powers, especially my Insight.

And I had faith in *myself*, which was no small feat. It had taken me a long time to get there, but I felt like I held within me the ability to accomplish something this difficult, and my Insight would guide me, step-by-step.

Or, that was the theory, anyway. And perhaps a shade of desperation helped me buy into it. Take my money, theory! Take it all!

We made the long walk down the peninsula to the castle, Donovan and I, hand-in-hand. I was inappropriately calm, given the situation. But maybe that goes to show how much fear in a given situation is simply created by not having made up one's mind about how one will act.

I'd made up my mind, and so everything else seemed unimportant.

I banged on the iron front doors, channeling Stu's authoritative knocks, and minutes later, Count Malavic opened up. He didn't say a word, only stared down his nose intensely at the three of us, putting together the pieces.

And then he threw his head back and laughed.

"Come to see the wizard?" he said.

Only I got the reference, of course. "Close. We're here to see the portal behind the curtain."

"I knew you'd be back," he said, still grinning, "but I hadn't guessed you'd bring *him* with you. Is this some sort of couples vacation? Vacationing to another realm to save the ex? Kinky, but I'm not judging. Just didn't know that's how you preferred it."

Ugh. The sooner we could get this over with, the better. "Are you going to invite us in?"

"I think you're confused who the vampire is here."

"That's not even a thing," I spat. Then I added, "Is it?"

"It is in your old world, but not here."

"The rules change from realm to realm?" For a brief moment, my faint understanding of magic was shaken to its core.

But the count said, "Of course not. However, my kindred living there like to say the rules are such because it creates a false sense of security that they can then exploit at will."

Sheesh. When people said Sebastian Malavic was one of the nicer vampires, they may not have been exaggerating after all. "The ploy doesn't work, though. People don't believe in vampires in my world."

"Maybe not in *Texas*"—he said the word like a slur—"but where I frequent, they do."

I considered taking the bait, but before I could ask him where he frequented, he said, "Why are you still standing there? Come on in." He stepped to the side, but not very far, meaning we had to enter single file and pass way too close to him.

What a creep.

He closed the door behind us and then lead the way

toward the staircase heading down into the dungeon-like study.

As we started our descent, Donovan said, "What happens when the rest of the High Council finds out about your portal? Or do you think they'll never find out?"

"You assume they don't already know," the count replied over his shoulder. "You assume I don't already have an agreement with them where they allow it to remain open so I have a place to properly hunt, and in return they keep it secret and continue receiving my monetary support for their public programs."

"No way," Donovan said. "Siobhan Astrid and I go way back. There's no way she would go along with this. At the very least, she would have told me about it."

"I'm sorry to be the one to break it to you that you are not as close with the elf as you've believed. Because she does know. But clearly she's smart enough not to let it become public knowledge."

"Is that what you use it for?" I said. "To cross into my world and hunt people?"

"Of course. But don't worry. I only prey upon willing victims, and I never kill them. Can't risk creating more of my kind. I'd be responsible for their care and would have to bring them back here, and then I would lose my coveted status as Eastwind's most rascally vamp."

This new revelation certainly didn't *decrease* my desire to close the portal.

Donovan, Grim, and I paused when we finally reached the bottom of the staircase. But Malavic glided on and unceremoniously yanked the curtain from the portal.

The light from it flooded the dark room. Through the gateway, it was either late dawn or early dusk, and the shadows from the visible tree stretched long.

When I was finally able to tear my eyes from it, I turned to Donovan, who was similarly transfixed.

Was he having second thoughts?

I'd been functioning under the assumption that he'd want it closed forever. Certainly, it benefitted him for me to no longer have the easy option to return to Tanner, but did that mean he was one hundred percent on board with the plan? After all, he'd lost the same people I had. He cared about them, too.

I saw him swallow hard before he jerked his head toward the count. "We're not going through. We're here to close it."

Count Malavic sneered at him. "Of *course* that's why you're here. I knew it the minute I saw the totality of your group darkening my doorstep. It's too bad all four of you don't appear to be of the same mind." He tsked. "You really should have come to a consensus before you came."

"You don't know what you're talking about," I said. "We have a consensus. And there are only three of us."

He moved away from the portal and took a seat in one of the nearby chairs. "There you are wrong. I smelled four distinct flavors of blood."

Could I have gotten some of Dmitri's blood on me back at the station?

I didn't have long to puzzle over that before Grim yelped and reared up onto his back legs. And in that moment, my breath caught in my chest as I discovered the true cause of his discomfort. He didn't have a crick in his neck, he had a Monster hitching a ride on his stomach.

"*No! Stop it! You promised!*" Grim shouted.

From the shaggy fur of his belly sprang the fluffy nightmare. And she made a beeline for the portal.

"Monster! No!" I shouted.

But she would never listen to me. Not when her witch was somewhere on the other side.

That's what real loyalty looks like, scolded a stern voice inside me.

Grim leaped and caught her in his jowls by the scruff of her neck a moment before she could make it through. I would have breathed a sigh of relief, but I decided instead to use my breath to shout at my familiar. "Why would you bring her?"

The munchkin cat flailed, screaming and clawing to get free.

"*She promised she wouldn't do anything rash. She said she just wanted to see it.*"

"For fang's sake! And you believed her?"

"*Of course not! That's why I was ready to pounce as soon as she—*" He yelped again when one of her swipes finally managed to catch him just under the eye, and that was all it took for her to wriggle free and dodge through the portal into another world.

"*Sweet baby jackalope!*"

I stood frozen in my spot next to Donovan. "Don't do it, Grim!" I didn't trust the look in his eyes.

"*She's my best friend! She's going to be eaten in under half an hour! I have to.*"

"But I'm your witch! You're going to choose her over

me?" Finally, my feet became unglued and I stomped forward, clapping my hands and shouting, "Bad dog!"

He tucked his tail and lowered his head.

"Do not go through that portal, you hear me? She made her choice!"

"And I've made mine." He sprang and I lunged for him in that same second, but I came up with nothing but a handful of his fur.

"No!" I yelled. "Grim! Come back!" But I wasn't sure he could hear me anymore.

It had happened so fast. Again. My gut clenched as I watched him disappear into the dense line of trees. I felt like I might throw up. My familiar had abandoned me.

Sebastian Malavic cackled madly, as well he should. For someone who loved a real swirlfest, he must have felt like he'd won the lottery.

The ugly realization crept in: I couldn't close the portal now. Being separated forever from Tanner was bad enough, but *Grim*? I wasn't even sure if I physically *could* intentionally do anything that would result in that. The same systems that allowed a witch to talk to her familiar surely had to have some failsafe that kept us from separating ourselves like that once we were bonded.

I couldn't speak, only stared unblinkingly at the place where Grim had just been. And then hands grabbed me and spun me around, and I was staring up into Donovan's endless blue eyes. "You have to."

"Have to *what*?" The sound of Malavic's maniacal laughter felt like a scalding poker in my brain, keeping me from understanding much of anything now.

But when Donovan kissed me, I understood what

he'd meant. The kiss said everything in a language I couldn't misinterpret.

How had it all gone so wrong? So terribly, terribly wrong? I'd made up my mind! I'd decided! And there I was, about to overrule myself.

I wanted the kiss to last forever, but I knew it wouldn't. I just didn't think it would end so soon.

He pulled away first. "I love you. More than I even knew I could. And we had more time together than I ever expected. I wouldn't change a thing."

"You wouldn't?"

He hesitated, then conceded, "Okay, I might. But now's not the time to get nitpicky, Nora. I'm trying to give a speech."

"Right. Sorry."

"You have to go."

"You're not coming with me."

"I can't leave Gustav behind."

"I know the feeling."

His arms tightened around me. "There's no way to know how this will turn out, but I'll wait for you. And if you don't want me when you come back…"

I wanted nothing more than to assure him that I still would, that nothing would have changed.

But I couldn't. I was going to find Tanner, and I knew myself too well.

"Come with me," I begged.

"I can't. Not now. I told you why." He let go of my arms and stepped back. "Be safe, Nora. Find our friends and bring them back."

I nodded, and stepped back from him, and it took all my willpower to tear my eyes away from his.

Then I shot one last dirty look at Malavic, called him an incredibly rude name from my own world, which I knew he'd understand, and stepped through the portal to chase after my hellion of a hellhound.

Epilogue

THREE DAYS LATER...

The truck slowed to a crawl, kicking up gravel from the road beneath its tires. My impromptu chauffeur, Steve, nodded at me from below his cowboy hat. "This is where we part ways." His skin was tanned and wrinkled from farm work, and I knew more about his family's deep roots in the South than I really cared to. But listening to him was the least I could do to thank him for a ride I had no way of paying for. And as any woman would know, keeping him happy kept me safe.

For someone who's already managed to die once, I have a pretty strong survival instinct.

When I opened the passenger-side door of the pickup, a feisty little munchkin cat sprang off my lap and landed soft as a feather on the ground.

"Don't forget that hound of yours," Steve said.

I forced another smile. "I couldn't if I tried."

I walked around to the back and undid the hatch.

"About time," Grim said as he leaped out of the bed. *"I think that ride jiggled a few teeth loose. People around here really use those buggies to get everywhere?"*

"It beats walking all that way," I said.

I gave Steve one last wave as he drove off, leaving us in a cloud of dust and exhaust.

"You spend two hours in the back where I was and I bet you'd change your mind."

I did feel for the poor guy. It was May in Southern Louisiana, and even though the sun had just dipped below the horizon, it was still hotter than a dragon's mouth, and about as humid.

"Come on, you two," I said, as Monster hopped onto her best friend's back. "Let's find us some water and a place to stay for the night."

Two days to locate Grim and Monster, and one day to find a ride this far south. I had no ID, no phone, and no money. And I was bone tired with miles to go.

But I did know where I could find Eva. Or at least I had a pretty good idea, and that was better than no idea.

We walked down the dark road toward the city, passing quietly beneath a thick canopy of trees. I was going back to where it all started, where I'd had a fight in a restaurant with a man I didn't care much about. Where I'd left in a hurry, speeding through the rain on the night I'd died.

We passed a sign reading, *New Orleans 2 miles.*

Not much farther, and then our search for our lost friends would officially begin.

FIRST-REALM PROBLEMS
Eastwind Witches 12

Nora is somewhere she never thought she'd see again: her old world. Desperate to bring Tanner and Eva back to Eastwind as soon as possible, she faces a major up-levee battle in New Orleans. Because without any money or a clear place to start, finding two witches in the city could require more magic than she alone possesses...

Nora's mysteries continue in
First-Realm Problems.

Grab your copy at
www.eastwindwitches.com/12

YOU'RE INVITED...

Join the Cozy Coven

**GET 1 NOVELLA AND 4 SHORT STORIES FROM
EASTWIND WHEN YOU SIGN UP**

Go to THECOZYCOVEN.COM

About the Author

Nova Nelson grew up on a steady diet of Agatha Christie novels. She loves the mind candy of cozy mysteries and has been weaving paranormal tales since she first learned handwriting. Those two loves meet in her Eastwind Witches series, and it's about time, if she does say so herself.

When she's not busy writing, she enjoys long walks with her strong-willed dogs and eating breakfast for dinner.

Say hello:
nova@novanelson.com